MAKERSPACE ENCYCLOPEDIAS

THE COOKING ENCYCLOPEDIA

BY ZOEY SCHRADER

Encyclopedias

An Imprint of Abdo Reference

abdobooks.com

TABLE OF CONTENTS

COOKING IS COOL

Welcome to the world of cooking! The cool thing about cooking is that you are the chef. You get to decide what to cook, how to cook, and what ingredients you want to use. A recipe can be different every time you make it. Cook a recipe just the way you like it. You can even share what you make with others. Being a cook is like being an artist in the kitchen. The most important ingredient is imagination!

Terrific Tortilla Soup

Night Before Egg Bake

Tasty Tex-Mex Tacos
Golden State
Potato Salad
Caramel French Toast

PREPARATION & SAFETY

A successful chef is smart, careful, and patient. Take time to review the basics before you start cooking. After that, get creative and have some fun!

ASK PERMISSION

- Before you cook, get permission to use the kitchen, cooking tools, and ingredients.
- If you'd like to do everything by yourself, say so. As long as you can do it safely, do it.
- When you need help, ask. Always get help when you use the stove or oven.

BE PREPARED

- Read through the entire recipe before you do anything else.
- Gather all your cooking tools and ingredients. Always wash fruits and vegetables. Rinse them well and pat them dry with a towel. Then they won't slip when you cut them.
- Get the ingredients ready. The list of ingredients includes preparation instructions. Some ingredients will have words such as chopped, sliced, or grated next to them. These words tell you how to prepare the ingredients. Give yourself plenty of time and be patient.

- Put each prepared ingredient into a separate bowl.
- Read the recipe instructions carefully. Do the steps in the order they are listed.

BE SMART, BE SAFE

- If you use the stove or oven, you need an adult in the kitchen with you. Never use the stove or oven if you are home alone!
- Always use oven mitts when handling hot pots and pans.
- Have an adult help with jobs such as draining boiling water. Also have an adult nearby when you are using a sharp tool such as a knife, peeler, or grater. Always use sharp tools with care.
- Always turn pot handles toward the back of the stove. This helps prevent accidental spills.
- Prevent accidents by working slowly and carefully. Take your time. If you get hurt, let an adult know right away!

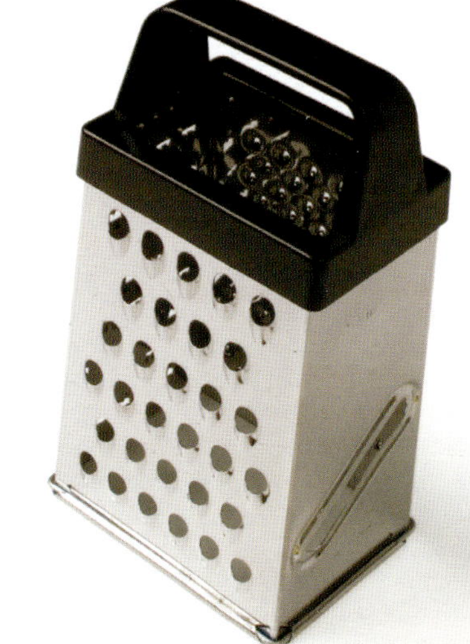

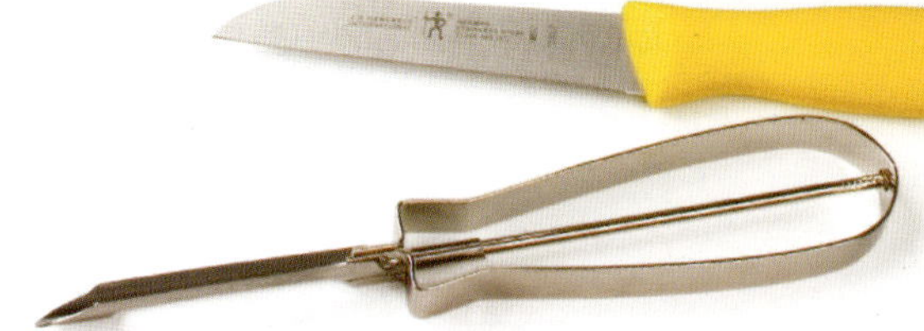

BE NEAT & CLEAN

- Start with clean hands, clean tools, and a clean work surface.
- Tie back long hair so it stays out of the way and out of the food.
- Wear comfortable clothing and roll up your sleeves. Aprons and chef hats are optional!

NO GERMS ALLOWED

After you handle raw eggs or raw meat, wash your hands with soap and water. Wash tools and work surfaces with soap and water too. Raw eggs and raw meat have bacteria that don't survive when the food is cooked. But the bacteria can survive at room or body temperature. These bacteria can make you very sick if you consume them. So, keep everything clean!

ALLERGY ALERT

Some people have allergic reactions when they eat certain kinds of food. An allergic reaction can require emergency medical help. Nut allergies are serious and can be especially dangerous. Before you serve anything made with nuts, ask if anyone has a nut allergy. People with nut allergies will not be able to eat what you have prepared. Don't be offended. It might save a life!

NOW THAT'S HOT!

Jalapeño peppers are very hot. Always wear rubber gloves when you chop jalapeño peppers. Then wash your hands, the cutting board, and the knife with soap and water right away. Be careful never to touch a cut pepper and then touch your eyes or nose.

CONVERSION CHART — INGREDIENTS

STANDARD	METRIC
¼ teaspoon	1.25 mL
½ teaspoon	2.5 mL
1 teaspoon	5 mL
1 tablespoon	15 mL
¼ cup	60 mL
⅓ cup	80 mL
½ cup	125 mL
⅔ cup	160 mL
¾ cup	175 mL
1 cup	240 mL
325°F	160°C
350°F	180°C
375°F	190°C
400°F	200°C

CONVERSION CHART — PAN SIZES

STANDARD	METRIC
8 × 8-inch	20 × 20-cm
9 × 9-inch	23 × 23-cm
9-inch round	23-cm round
9 × 5-inch	23 × 13-cm
9 × 13-inch	23 × 33-cm

8 × 8-inch cake pan

measuring spoons

measuring cups

saucepan

COOL COOKING TERMS

Learn basic cooking terms and the actions that go with them. Whenever you need to remind yourself, just turn back to these pages.

BEAT

Beat means to mix well using a whisk or an electric mixer.

BOIL

Boil means to heat liquid until it begins to bubble.

BREAKING AN EGG

Tap the widest part of the egg firmly against the side of a bowl until a crack goes through the shell and inner membrane. Hold the cracked egg over a bowl. Pull the two sides of the shell apart. Let the egg white and yolk fall into the bowl. Discard the shell. Remove any shell pieces that fall into the bowl.

CHOP

Chop means to cut things into small pieces. If a recipe says finely chopped, it means you need very small pieces. When you slice or chop round foods, such as carrots, cut a lengthwise slice off one side. Put the flat side on the cutting board. Then the food won't roll when you cut it.

COAT

Coat means to cover something with another ingredient or mixture.

CORE

Core means to remove the core and seeds from a fruit, usually an apple. Use a tool called a corer to make this job easier. Put a clean apple on a cutting board and center the corer over the middle of it. Press the corer all the way through the apple until it hits the cutting board. Twist the corer to loosen the core and seeds. Then pull the corer back out of the apple. The core and seeds will come out of the apple when you pull out the corer.

CRUSH

Crush means to break something into crumbs with a rolling pin.

CUBE OR DICE

Cube or dice means to cut cube-shaped or dice-shaped pieces. Usually dice refers to smaller pieces, and cube refers to larger pieces. Often a recipe will give you a dimension, such as ¼-inch (0.6-cm) dice. Use two steps to dice or cube. First make all your cuts going one direction. Then turn the cutting board and make the crosscuts.

CUT IN

Cut in refers to working butter into dry ingredients. You can use a pastry blender or two table knives to do this. Cut the butter into small pieces to work it into the flour mixture. The mixture will look like small, even crumbs.

DRAIN

Drain means to remove liquid using a strainer or colander.

DRIZZLE

Drizzle means to slowly pour a liquid over something.

FOLD

Fold means to gently mix ingredients together. Use a silicone spatula or a mixing spoon to lift and turn the mixture just until it is blended. Don't overdo it!

GRATE

Grate means to shred something into small pieces using a grater. A grater has surfaces covered in holes with raised, sharp edges. You rub the food against a surface using firm pressure.

GREASE

Grease means to coat a surface of a pan or dish with non-stick cooking spray, oil, or butter to keep food from sticking to it. Use a wad of waxed paper or paper towel to spread a light layer of grease evenly over the pan.

JUICE

To juice a fruit means to remove the juice from its insides by squeezing it or using a juicer.

KNEAD

Knead means to use your hands to make dough smooth. Fold the dough in half and press down on it. Turn the dough sideways, fold it in half again, and press down on it again. Continue to turn, fold, and press the dough until it is smooth.

GET FRESH!

Dried herbs are stronger than fresh herbs. If you substitute fresh herbs for dried herbs, use at least three times as much as the recipe calls for. For example, if the recipe says 1 teaspoon dried basil, use 3 teaspoons chopped fresh basil.

MARINATE

Marinate means to soak food in a seasoned liquid.

MASH

Mash means to use the back of a fork to press down and smash the food into a paste. You can use a potato masher if you need to mash a large quantity.

MEASURE

Most ingredients are measured by the cup, tablespoon, or teaspoon. Measuring cups and spoons come in a variety of sizes. An amount is printed or etched on each one to show how much it holds. To measure ½ cup, use the measuring cup marked ½ cup and fill it to the top. To measure flour, spoon flour into a measuring cup. Fill the measuring cup to overflowing. Then use a table knife to scrape the excess flour back into the bag or canister. Ingredients such as meat and cheese are measured by weight in ounces or pounds (grams or kilograms). You purchase them by weight too.

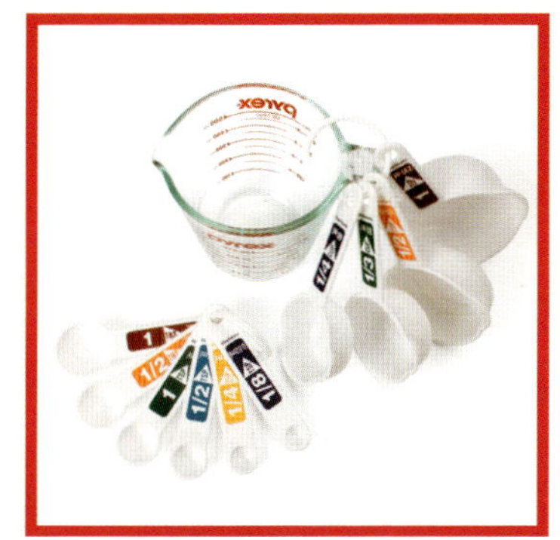

TRY THIS

Set a measuring cup inside a large bowl to catch spills. Hold a measuring spoon over a small bowl or cup to catch spills.

MINCE

Mince means to cut the food into the tiniest possible pieces. Garlic is often minced and sometimes onion is too.

MIX

When you mix, you stir ingredients together, usually with a large spoon.

PAT

Pat means to press down gently using your hands. To pat a mixture into a pan, use your hands to press it into a smooth layer.

PEEL

Peel means to remove the skin. Use a peeler for carrots, potatoes, and more. Hold the item to be peeled against the cutting board. Slide the peeler away from you along the surface of the food. To peel onion or garlic, remove the papery shell. Trim each end with a knife. Peel off the outer layer with your fingers.

SAUTÉ

Sauté means to cook using a small amount of grease in a shallow pan over high heat.

SEPARATE AN EGG

When a recipe calls for an egg yolk, you need to separate the yolk from the egg white. Crack the egg into a small bowl. Use a slotted spoon to gently lift the yolk from the bowl.

SHRED

Shred means to tear or cut into small pieces.

SIMMER

Simmer means to cook something so it bubbles gently.

SLICE

Slice means to cut food into pieces of the same thickness.

SOAK

Soak means to let something sit in a liquid.

SPREAD

Spread means to smooth an ingredient across a surface. Use a knife or a silicone spatula to spread creamy ingredients into a smooth, even layer.

SALT & PEPPER TO TASTE?

Some recipes say to add salt and pepper to taste. This means you should rely on your taste buds. Take a small spoonful of the food and taste it. If it isn't as salty as you like, add a little salt. If it needs more pepper, add some. Then mix and taste it again.

SPRINKLE

Sprinkle means to drop small pieces of something.

TOSS

Toss means to turn ingredients over to coat them with seasonings.

WHISK

Whisk means to beat quickly by hand. The tool you use to whisk is also called a whisk.

Move the whisk using a circular motion. If you don't have a whisk, you can use a fork instead.

ZEST

Zest means to make fine shavings of the outer layer of a citrus fruit. The shavings are also called zest. You zest citrus fruit by rubbing it over the smallest holes on a grater or over a tool called a zester. Grate only the colored layer of the skin. This layer contains flavorful oils. The white layer beneath the colored layer, called the pith, is bitter and should not be grated.

MAKE A GOOD MATCH!

Have fun and invent your own recipes by substituting one ingredient for another. Use the same amount of the substitute ingredient as the one it is replacing. The only thing you need to remember is to make a good match. It is best to make substitutions with dry ingredients, fruits, or vegetables. For example, if you prefer red peppers to green peppers, go ahead and use them. If a recipe calls for pepperoni, try using sausage instead.

BREAKFASTS

Want to get your day off to a great start? Breakfasts such as smoothies, scrambled eggs, and parfaits are quick and easy to make. Some dishes can be prepared ahead of time so they're ready to go when your morning alarm goes off! Other recipes can be made the night before and baked in the morning for a delicious hot breakfast.

Pork Sausage Rolls

Great Granola

Crazy Cranberry Scones
Perfect Bacon Pancakes
Razzleberry Smoothies

PERFECT SCRAMBLED EGGS

makes 4 servings

INGREDIENTS

8 eggs
½ cup milk
¼ teaspoon salt
⅛ teaspoon pepper
3 tablespoons butter

TOOLS & EQUIPMENT

mixing bowl
measuring cups
measuring spoons
whisk
skillet
mixing spoon or silicone spatula

1. Break the eggs into a mixing bowl.
2. Add the milk, salt, and pepper and whisk until blended. For fluffier eggs, whisk for 1 more minute.
3. Melt the butter in a skillet over medium heat. When the butter is foamy, pour the egg mixture into the skillet.
4. Use a mixing spoon or a silicone spatula to gently stir the eggs as they cook. When the eggs are cooked through, serve them immediately.

TRY THIS

Stir 4 ounces (113 g) of cubed cream cheese into the eggs while they are cooking. Top the eggs with sliced scallions, chopped fresh parsley, or grated cheese.

PORK SAUSAGE ROLLS

makes 4 servings

INGREDIENTS

2 sheets premade puff pastry
4 tablespoons mustard
8 pork sausages
1 egg

1. Preheat the oven to 350 degrees. Cover the baking sheet with aluminum foil. Set the sheet aside.
2. Cut each puff pastry sheet in half diagonally. Brush mustard on top of each pastry.
3. Roll each pastry around a sausage. Pinch the edges of the pastry closed.
4. Place the rolls on the baking sheet. Crack the egg in a small bowl and whisk it. Brush the outside of each roll with egg.
5. Bake for 15 minutes, or until the pastry is golden brown.

TOOLS & EQUIPMENT

baking sheet
aluminum foil
knife
cutting board
measuring spoon
basting brush
mixing bowl
whisk

NIGHT BEFORE EGG BAKE

makes 6 to 8 servings

INGREDIENTS

- 2 tablespoons butter, plus extra
- ½ pound (0.23 kg) sourdough bread, cut into 1-inch (2.5-cm) cubes
- 1 or 2 bell peppers, chopped (you can use red, green, or both)
- 8 chopped scallions
- 8 large eggs
- 3 cups whole milk
- 1½ teaspoons salt
- 2 teaspoons dry mustard
- 2 to 3 cups diced ham
- 1½ cups grated cheddar cheese

1. Preheat the oven to 300 degrees. Grease the baking dish with butter.
2. Put the bread cubes on the baking sheet. Put the sheet in the oven for 10 minutes.
3. Heat the butter in a skillet over medium-high heat. Add the bell peppers and scallions. Sauté for 3 minutes. Set the skillet aside.
4. Whisk the eggs, milk, salt, and mustard together in a large bowl. Stir in the vegetables.
5. Arrange the bread cubes evenly in the baking dish. Sprinkle the ham over the bread. Pour the egg mixture over everything. Cover with plastic wrap and refrigerate overnight.
6. Preheat the oven to 375 degrees. Uncover the dish and bake for 50 minutes. Sprinkle the cheese over the top. Bake for 10 more minutes, or until the middle is set. Let it cool for 10 minutes before serving.

TOOLS & EQUIPMENT

serrated knife
cutting board
knife
grater
9 × 13-inch baking dish
baking sheet
skillet
spatula
whisk
measuring cups
measuring spoons
mixing bowl
plastic wrap

RAZZLEBERRY SMOOTHIES

makes 2 smoothies

INGREDIENTS

1 cup frozen raspberries
1 cup raspberry yogurt
1 cup orange juice
1 teaspoon superfine sugar

TOOLS & EQUIPMENT

measuring cups
measuring spoon
blender
two large glasses

1. Let the frozen raspberries thaw for 20 minutes.
2. Put all of the ingredients in a blender. Blend on high speed until the ingredients are smooth, about 1 minute.
3. Pour the smoothie into two large glasses and serve.

TRY THIS

You can also make a smoothie with fresh fruit! Use 1½ cups of fresh fruit, 1 cup of yogurt, ½ cup of juice, 1 teaspoon of superfine sugar, and a few ice cubes. Blend until the ice is crushed and the mixture is smooth.

RAINBOW FRUIT SALAD

makes 6 servings

INGREDIENTS

- 1 cup green grapes
- 1 cup red grapes
- 1 cup sliced strawberries
- 1 cup cantaloupe, cut in 1-inch (2.5-cm) cubes
- 1 cup honeydew melon, cut in 1-inch (2.5-cm) cubes
- 1 cup pineapple, cut in 1-inch (2.5-cm) cubes
- 1 cup blueberries
- juice from 1 orange
- 2 teaspoons superfine sugar

1. Put all the fruit in a bowl. Set the bowl aside.
2. Squeeze the juice from an orange using a juicer. Pick any seeds from the juice, then pour the juice over the fruit.
3. Sprinkle the sugar over the fruit and mix well.
4. Chill the salad in the refrigerator for at least 1 hour before serving.

TOOLS & EQUIPMENT

knife
cutting board
measuring cups
mixing bowl
juicer
measuring spoon
spoon

TRY THIS

Use any fruit you like! Just cut it into bite-size pieces and add it to the mix. Raspberries and blackberries do not need to be cut. When using cherries, remove the pits. If you use bananas or apples, brush the cut surfaces with lemon juice so they won't turn brown.

CRAZY CRANBERRY SCONES

makes 8 scones

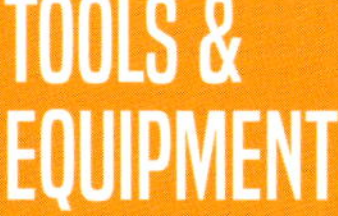

TOOLS & EQUIPMENT

baking sheet
parchment paper
whisk
mixing bowls
measuring cups
measuring spoons
table knife
pastry blender
zester or grater
fork
waxed paper
pastry brush
wire rack

INGREDIENTS

- 2 cups all-purpose flour
- ⅓ cup plus 1 tablespoon sugar
- 1 tablespoon baking powder
- ½ teaspoon salt
- 6 tablespoons cold butter
- ⅔ cup dried cranberries
- 1 teaspoon orange zest
- 1 egg
- ½ cup plus 1 tablespoon heavy cream

1. Preheat the oven to 425 degrees. Line the baking sheet with parchment paper.
2. Whisk the flour, ⅓ cup of sugar, baking powder, and salt together in a large mixing bowl.
3. Cut the butter into ½-inch (1.3-cm) cubes using a table knife. Add it to the flour mixture in the mixing bowl.
4. Use a pastry blender to cut the butter into the flour mixture. Work the mixture until it forms pea-size pieces. The texture needs to be coarse, so do not make a paste or a smooth mixture!
5. Add the cranberries and orange zest to the bowl and mix them in with a fork. Set this bowl aside.
6. Mix the egg and ½ cup of cream in a small mixing bowl with a fork. Add the egg mixture to the large mixing bowl and stir with a fork until everything is moistened.
7. Use your hands to work the mixture into a ball. Knead the dough about 10 times in the bowl. Move the ball of dough to a sheet of waxed paper.
8. Use your hands to flatten the dough ball into a circle about 10 inches (25 cm) across. Cut it into 8 wedges using a table knife.
9. Put the wedges on the baking sheet and brush the tops with the remaining 1 tablespoon of cream. Sprinkle the remaining 1 tablespoon of sugar over the tops.
10. Bake the scones for 12 minutes, or until the tops are lightly browned. Cool them on a wire rack.

GREAT GRANOLA

makes about 10 cups

INGREDIENTS

- 5 cups rolled oats
- 1 cup flaked coconut
- 1 cup cashew pieces
- 1 cup sunflower seeds
- ½ cup wheat germ
- ½ cup sesame seeds
- ⅔ cup brown sugar
- ⅓ cup honey
- ⅔ cup cooking oil
- 1½ cups raisins
- milk (optional)
- sliced fruit (optional)

TOOLS & EQUIPMENT

- measuring cups
- mixing bowl
- saucepan
- silicone spatula
- baking sheet
- aluminum foil
- mixing spoon

1. Preheat the oven to 325 degrees.
2. Mix the oats, coconut, cashews, sunflower seeds, wheat germ, and sesame seeds in a large mixing bowl.
3. Put the brown sugar and honey in a saucepan. Cook over medium heat, stirring constantly until the sugar dissolves.
4. Pour the sugar mixture and oil over the oat mixture. Mix with a silicone spatula until the mixture is coated.
5. Spread the mixture on a baking sheet. To keep the granola from burning, keep it away from the sides of the baking sheet.
6. Bake for 40 minutes. Every 10 minutes, remove the pan from the oven and stir the mixture so it bakes evenly. Remember to keep the granola away from the sides of the pan. The granola will be golden brown when it is done.
7. Remove the pan from the oven and spread the granola on foil with a mixing spoon to cool.
8. When the granola is cool, put it in a large mixing bowl and mix in the raisins.
9. Serve the granola topped with milk and, if you like, sliced fresh fruit.

PERFECT BACON PANCAKES

makes 4 servings

INGREDIENTS

2 strips bacon
¾ cup buttermilk
1 cup flour
2 tablespoons sugar
1 teaspoon baking powder
½ teaspoon baking soda
½ teaspoon salt
½ teaspoon vanilla extract
1 egg
non-stick cooking spray

1. Preheat the oven to 400 degrees. Line the baking sheet with aluminum foil. Put the bacon strips on the sheet. Bake for 15 minutes or until the bacon is golden brown. Turn the strips over halfway through.
2. Place the bacon on paper towels to drain. Break the bacon strips in half once they have cooled.
3. Put the buttermilk, flour, sugar, baking powder, baking soda, salt, vanilla extract, and egg in the mixing bowl. Whisk the ingredients together. Pour the mixture into a glass measuring cup.
4. Grease the frying pan with non-stick spray. Set the heat to medium.
5. Pour about ¼ cup of the pancake batter into the frying pan. Press a bacon strip into the batter. Cook it until the batter bubbles.
6. Flip the pancake. Cook it until both sides are golden brown.
7. Repeat steps 5 and 6 with the remaining batter.

TOOLS & EQUIPMENT

baking sheet
aluminum foil
spatula
paper towels
measuring cups
measuring spoons
mixing bowl
whisk
glass measuring cup
frying pan

CARAMEL FRENCH TOAST

makes 6 servings

INGREDIENTS

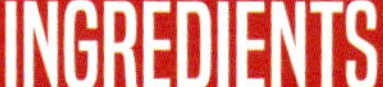

½ cup butter, plus extra
⅔ cup brown sugar
1 tablespoon sugar
2 teaspoons cinnamon
bread, cut into ¾-inch (1.9-cm) slices
6 eggs
1¾ cups whole milk

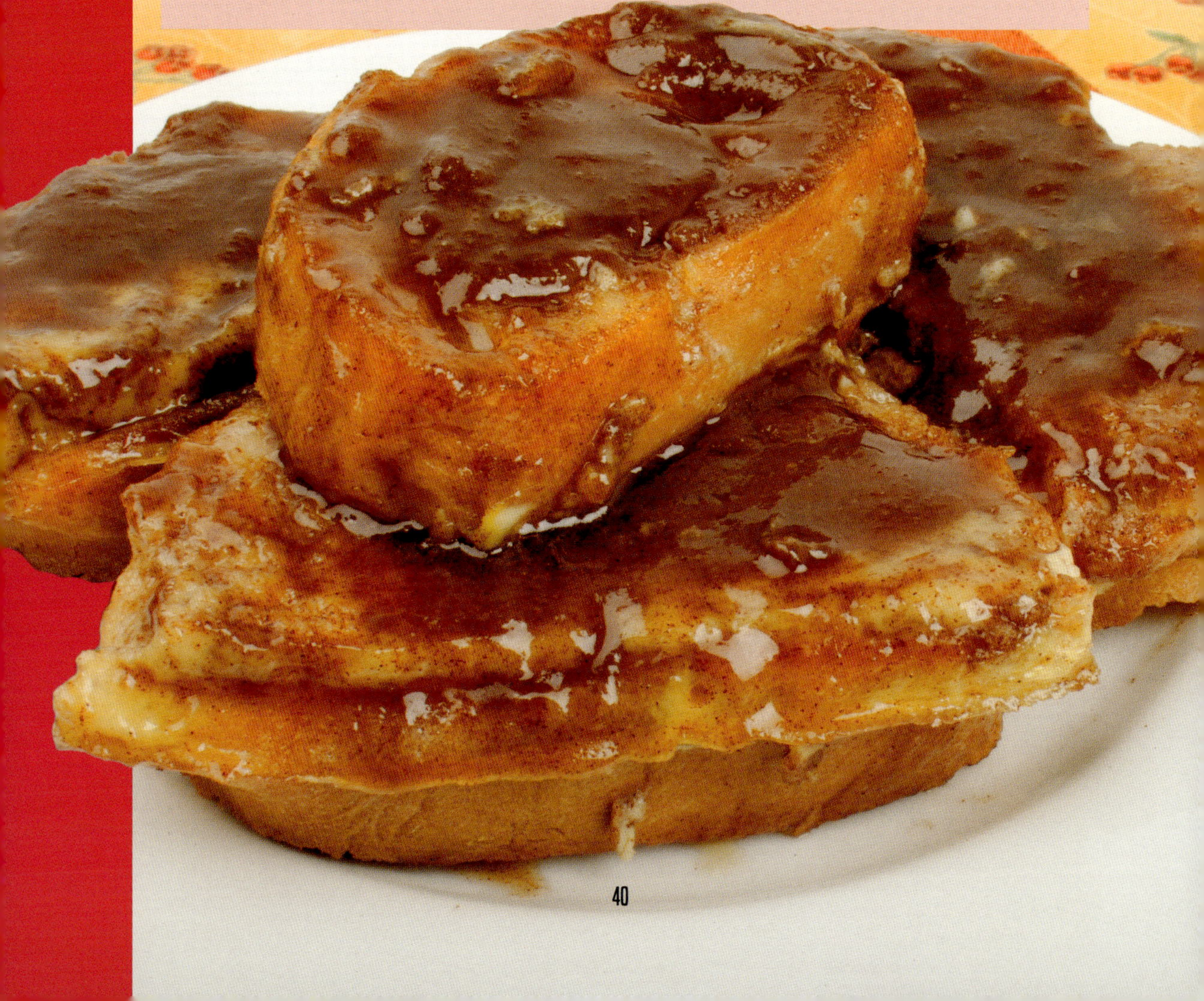

1. Preheat the oven to 350 degrees. Grease the baking dish with butter.
2. To make the caramel, melt ½ cup butter in a small saucepan. Add the sugars and cook over medium heat. Stir constantly until the sugars are dissolved and the mixture is bubbling. Remove from heat and stir in the cinnamon.
3. Pour the caramel into the baking dish. Arrange bread slices in a single layer on top.
4. Whisk the eggs and milk together in a mixing bowl. Pour it evenly over the bread slices.
5. Bake for 30 minutes. Flip the pieces of bread over when you serve them so the caramel will be on top.

TOOLS & EQUIPMENT

serrated knife
cutting board
9 × 13-inch baking dish
saucepan
measuring cups
measuring spoons
mixing spoon
mixing bowl
whisk

SOUR CREAM COFFEE CAKE

makes 12 servings

INGREDIENTS

FOR THE COFFEE CAKE

- ½ cup butter at room temperature, plus extra
- 2 cups all-purpose flour, plus extra
- 1 teaspoon baking powder
- 1 teaspoon baking soda
- ½ teaspoon salt
- 1 cup sugar
- 2 eggs
- 1 cup sour cream
- 1 teaspoon vanilla extract

FOR THE TOPPING

- ½ cup sugar
- ½ cup brown sugar
- 1 tablespoon cinnamon
- 1 cup chopped walnuts or pecans (optional)

1. Preheat the oven to 325 degrees. Grease the baking dish with butter. Sprinkle flour over the inside of the dish. Turn the dish upside down to remove any extra flour.
2. Combine the baking powder, baking soda, salt, and 2 cups flour in a small mixing bowl.
3. Put the butter and sugar in a large mixing bowl. Beat with an electric mixer until it's creamy and light. Add the eggs, sour cream, and vanilla extract. Stir well. Add the flour mixture and stir until smooth.
4. Spread the batter in the baking dish. The batter will be very thick. Use a silicone spatula to spread it evenly. If you wet the silicone spatula with water, the batter will be easier to spread.
5. Stir the topping ingredients together in a small mixing bowl.
6. Sprinkle the topping mixture over the batter.
7. Bake for 30 minutes. Stick a toothpick into the center of the cake. If it comes out clean, the cake is done. If not, bake for a few more minutes and test again.

TOOLS & EQUIPMENT

9 × 13-inch baking dish
measuring cups
measuring spoons
mixing bowls
mixing spoon
electric mixer
silicone spatula
toothpick

MAIN DISHES

The main dish is the most important part of any meal. Choose a dish to be your centerpiece. Then choose side dishes, desserts, and more to go with the main dish!

Classic Croque
Monsieur
Philly Cheesesteak Sandwich
Legendary
Lasagna
Delectable
Mac & Cheese

TASTY BASIC BURGER

makes 4 burgers

INGREDIENTS

- 1 pound (0.45 kg) ground beef
- 1 egg
- ⅓ cup dry breadcrumbs
- ½ teaspoon pepper
- 2 teaspoons Worcestershire sauce
- vegetable oil
- salt
- 4 hamburger buns

1. Have an adult helper preheat the grill to medium-high heat.
2. Put the ground beef, egg, breadcrumbs, pepper, and Worcestershire sauce in a mixing bowl. Mix with your hands until well blended.
3. Divide the mixture into fourths. Shape each piece into a patty ¾ inches (1.9 cm) thick. Make a small dent in the center to keep the patty from swelling.
4. Lightly grease the grate with oil. Place the patties on the grill. Sprinkle them with salt. Cook the patties for 5 to 7 minutes on each side. Serve them on buns with all your favorite toppings.

TOOLS & EQUIPMENT

measuring spoons
measuring cups
mixing bowl
grill spatula

CHICAGO-STYLE HOT DOGS

makes 8 Chicago dogs

INGREDIENTS

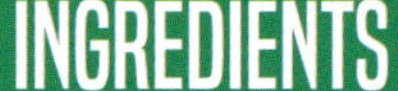

- 8 all-beef hot dogs
- 8 hot dog buns
- yellow mustard
- ½ cup sweet green pickle relish
- ½ cup finely chopped onion
- 16 sport peppers
- 3 tomatoes, cut into 8 wedges
- 8 dill pickle spears
- celery salt

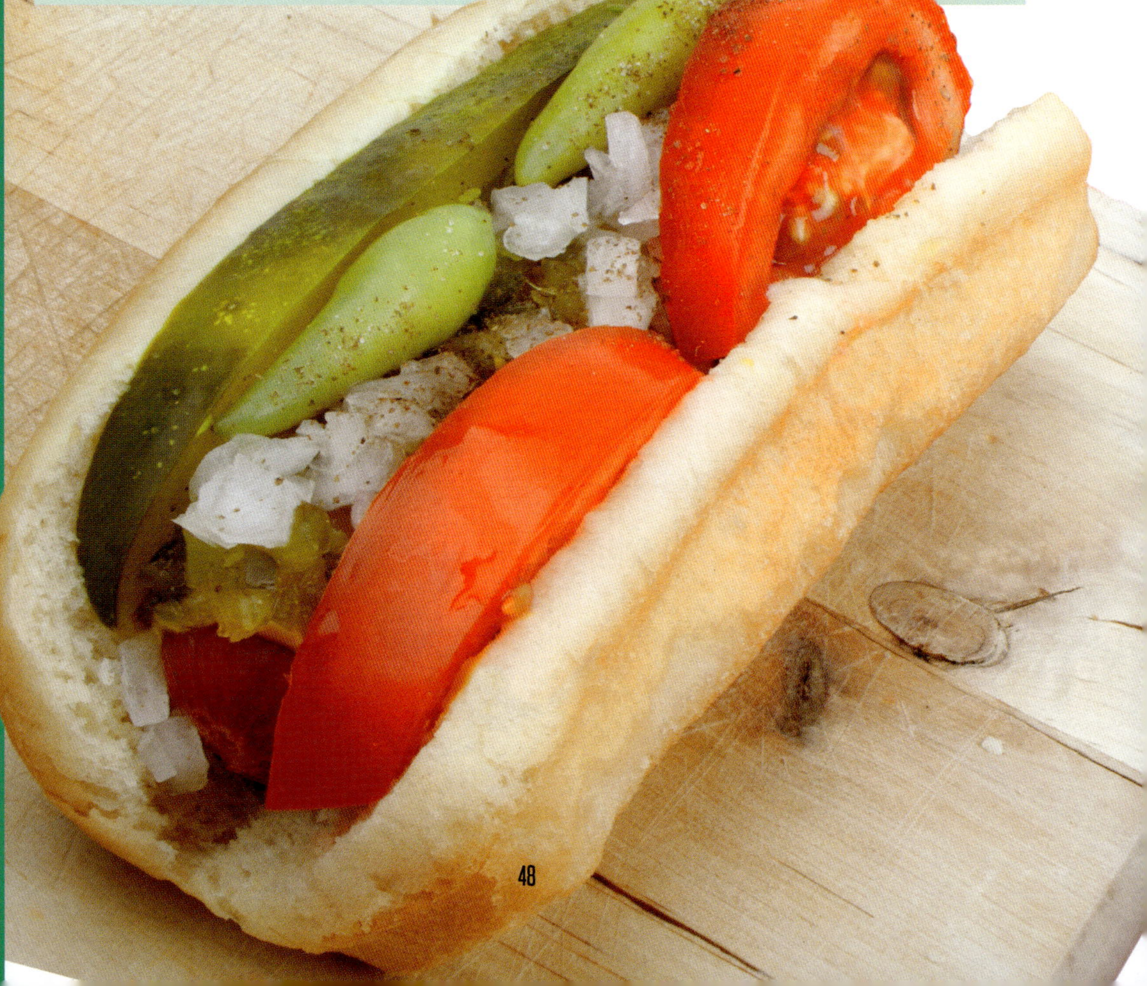

1. Bring a saucepan of water to a boil. Turn the heat to low and add the hot dogs. Heat the hot dogs for 5 minutes. Use tongs to remove the hot dogs and place them on a plate.
2. Carefully pour out all but 1 inch (2.5 cm) of water. Put a steamer basket in the pan. Put the buns in the steamer basket and cover the pot. Steam the buns for 2 minutes or until warm. Use tongs to remove the buns.
3. Put a hot dog in each bun. Put the toppings on in this order: yellow mustard, 1 tablespoon sweet green pickle relish, 1 tablespoon chopped onion, 2 sport peppers, tomato wedges on one side of the hot dog, pickle spears on the other side of the hot dog, and a sprinkle of celery salt.

TOOLS & EQUIPMENT

measuring cups	saucepan with lid	steamer basket
knife	tongs	measuring spoons
cutting board	plate	

MARINATED VEGGIE KEBABS

makes 6 servings

INGREDIENTS

- ½ cup olive oil
- ½ cup fresh lemon juice
- 3 cloves garlic, minced
- salt and pepper
- 2 zucchini, cut into ½-inch (1.3-cm) slices
- 1 yellow squash, cut into ½-inch (1.3-cm) slices
- 1 green or red bell pepper, cut into 1-inch (2.5-cm) pieces
- 12 cherry tomatoes
- 1 red or white onion, cut into wedges
- vegetable oil

TOOLS & EQUIPMENT

- knife
- cutting board
- juicer
- measuring cups
- mixing bowl
- whisk
- bamboo skewers
- 9 × 13-inch baking dish
- plastic wrap
- grill tongs

1. To make the marinade, whisk the olive oil, lemon juice, and garlic together in a mixing bowl until well blended. If the marinade is too sour, add more olive oil and whisk to blend. Add salt and pepper to taste.
2. Put the vegetables on the skewers.
3. Place the kebabs in the baking dish. Pour the marinade over the kebabs. Turn the kebabs to coat the vegetables. Cover the dish with plastic wrap and let sit for 30 to 60 minutes.
4. Have an adult helper preheat the grill to medium heat.
5. Lightly grease the grate with vegetable oil. Place the kebabs on the grill. Cook for 8 to 10 minutes. Turn them often to prevent burning. Cook until the vegetables are tender but not mushy.

TRY THIS

Twist the skewer as you push it gently through the cut vegetables. This helps keep the vegetables from splitting.

CRISPY FISH & CHIPS

makes 4 servings

INGREDIENTS

- 2 potatoes
- 2 tablespoons vegetable oil
- 1 egg
- 1 tablespoon lemon juice
- ¾ cup breadcrumbs
- ¼ cup grated Parmesan cheese
- 1 pound (0.45 kg) cod fillets, cut into strips

1. Preheat the oven to 325 degrees. Cover the baking sheets with aluminum foil.
2. Cut the potatoes into ¼-inch (0.6-cm) slices. Put them in a bowl. Add the oil and stir to coat the potatoes. Put the potatoes on a baking sheet.
3. Whisk the egg and lemon juice together in a bowl.
4. Put the breadcrumbs and cheese on a plate. Coat the fish strips with the egg mixture. Then roll them in the breadcrumb mixture. Pat the strips gently so the breadcrumbs stick. Put the fish on the other baking sheet.
5. Put both baking sheets in the oven. Take the fish out after 30 minutes. Leave the potatoes in the oven for 10 more minutes.

TOOLS & EQUIPMENT

knife
cutting board
juicer
grater
baking sheets
aluminum foil
measuring spoons
mixing bowls
whisk
measuring cups
plate

BUFFALO CHICKEN WINGS

makes 5 servings

INGREDIENTS

- ½ cup flour
- ¼ teaspoon paprika
- ¼ teaspoon cayenne pepper
- ¼ teaspoon salt
- 10 chicken wings
- non-stick cooking spray
- ⅔ cup butter
- ⅓ cup hot sauce
- celery sticks (optional)
- ranch dressing (optional)

1. Put the flour, paprika, cayenne pepper, and salt in a bowl. Stir them together. Put the flour mixture and the wings in the plastic bag. Shake it to coat the chicken. Refrigerate it for 90 minutes.
2. Preheat the oven to 350 degrees. Put the rack on the baking sheet. Put the wings on the rack. Bake them for 45 minutes.
3. Turn the oven to 375 degrees. Take the wings out of the oven. Coat them with cooking spray. Bake for 20 more minutes.
4. Take the wings out of the oven. Cut into a wing. If it's pink inside, bake the wings a little longer. When done, remove the wings from the oven.
5. Put the butter in a microwave-safe bowl. Microwave it on low for 1 minute. Stir in the hot sauce. Coat the wings with the sauce. Try serving the wings with a side of celery sticks and ranch dressing!

TOOLS & EQUIPMENT

measuring cups
measuring spoons
mixing bowls
mixing spoon
large plastic zipper bag
baking rack
baking sheet
tongs
knife
cutting board
microwave-safe bowl

CRUNCHY CHICKEN STRIPS

makes 4 servings

INGREDIENTS

- 2 teaspoons salt
- 2 teaspoons pepper
- 2 pounds (0.9 kg) chicken breast, sliced
- ⅓ cup orange juice
- ½ cup sweetened condensed milk
- 1 egg
- 1⅓ cups crushed cornflakes
- 1 cup shredded coconut
- vegetable oil

1. Place the chicken on a plate. Sprinkle salt and pepper on both sides of the chicken slices.
2. Put the orange juice, sweetened condensed milk, and egg in a bowl. Whisk them together. Put the cornflakes and coconut in another bowl. Stir them together.
3. Dip the chicken slices in the orange juice mixture. Then coat them with the cornflake mixture.
4. Put 2 inches (5 cm) of oil in the frying pan. Heat the oil on medium-high. Fry the chicken for 3 to 4 minutes on one side. Turn the chicken over. Fry it for 3 to 4 more minutes. Lay a paper towel on a clean plate. Place the chicken on the plate. Let it cool.

TOOLS & EQUIPMENT

knife
cutting board
plates
measuring spoons
measuring cups
mixing bowls
whisk
mixing spoon
tongs
frying pan
paper towels

CHEESY BLT PIZZA

makes 8 servings

INGREDIENTS

- 12 strips bacon
- ¾ cup sour cream
- ¼ cup mayonnaise
- 8 ounces (227 g) cream cheese
- 1 package ranch dip mix
- 2 16-ounce (454-g) premade pizza crusts
- 2 cups grated mozzarella cheese
- ½ onion, chopped
- 2 tomatoes, diced
- 1 cup shredded lettuce

1. Preheat the oven to 400 degrees. Line the baking sheet with aluminum foil.
2. Put the bacon strips on the sheet. Bake for 15 minutes or until the bacon is golden brown. Turn the strips over halfway through.
3. Place the bacon on paper towels to drain.
4. Chop the bacon into small pieces.
5. Preheat the oven to 425 degrees. Put the sour cream, mayonnaise, cream cheese, and dip mix in a large bowl. Stir the ingredients together.
6. Put a pizza crust on the pizza pan. Spread half of the sour cream mixture over the pizza crust.
7. Sprinkle half of the mozzarella cheese, onion, tomatoes, and bacon on the pizza. Bake for 10 minutes.
8. Take the pizza out of the oven. Sprinkle half of the lettuce on top.
9. Repeat steps 7 through 9 to make a second pizza.

TOOLS & EQUIPMENT

knife
cutting board
grater
baking sheet
aluminum foil
spatula
paper towels
measuring cups
mixing bowl
mixing spoon
pizza pan
silicone spatula

DELECTABLE MAC & CHEESE

makes 8 servings

INGREDIENTS

non-stick cooking spray
16-ounce (454-g) package elbow macaroni
1½ cups grated mozzarella cheese
1 cup grated cheddar cheese
½ cup grated Parmesan cheese
½ cup grated Swiss cheese
½ cup ricotta cheese
½ cup sour cream
¾ cup heavy cream
1 tablespoon chopped parsley
½ teaspoon garlic salt

TOOLS & EQUIPMENT

grater
9 × 13-inch baking dish
saucepan
colander
measuring cups
mixing bowls
mixing spoon
small bowl
measuring spoons

1. Preheat the oven to 400 degrees. Grease the baking dish with non-stick cooking spray.
2. Fill a large saucepan with water. Bring it to a boil. Add the macaroni. Cook for 6 minutes. Drain the macaroni and set it aside.
3. Put the mozzarella, cheddar, Parmesan, and Swiss cheeses in a mixing bowl. Stir. Set ½ cup of the cheese mixture aside in a small bowl for the topping.

4. Put the ricotta cheese, sour cream, heavy cream, parsley, and garlic salt in a separate mixing bowl. Stir well. Add the ricotta mixture to the cheese mixture.
5. Stir in the macaroni. Spread the mixture evenly in the baking dish. Sprinkle the ½ cup cheese mixture on top.
6. Bake for 10 minutes or until the cheese is melted. Turn the oven to broil. Broil for 5 minutes to brown the top.

TASTY TEX-MEX TACOS

Makes 12 tacos

INGREDIENTS

12 taco shells

TO MAKE THE FILLING

1 pound (0.45 kg) ground beef or turkey

1 cup chopped white onion

1 clove garlic, minced

8-ounce (227-g) can tomato sauce

⅓ cup water

¾ teaspoon salt

1 tablespoon chili powder

½ teaspoon dried oregano

½ teaspoon ground cumin

FOR THE GARNISHES

½ head iceberg lettuce, cut in ¼-inch (0.6-cm) strips

1 large tomato, diced

1 cup salsa or pico de gallo

1½ cups grated cheese (cheddar or Colby-Jack)

1. Put the ground meat, onion, and garlic in a frying pan. Cook over medium-high heat. As the meat browns, break it up with a mixing spoon so it cooks evenly. Cook until all the pink color is gone from the meat.
2. Have an adult helper drain the grease from the pan.
3. Stir in the tomato sauce, water, salt, and spices. Cook over medium heat for 5 to 10 minutes, stirring occasionally. Put the meat filling in a bowl and set the bowl aside.
4. Put the taco shells on a baking sheet. Warm the shells in a preheated, 350-degree oven for 3 minutes.
5. Remove the shells from the oven and use tongs to gently put them on a platter.
6. Put 2 tablespoons of the meat filling in each shell. Take the serving platter to the table.
7. Put bowls of lettuce, tomato, salsa, and cheese on the table. Let everyone make their own tacos using the garnishes they like best.

TOOLS & EQUIPMENT

knife
cutting board
grater
measuring cups
frying pan
mixing spoon
measuring spoons
baking sheet
tongs
serving platter
serving bowls

BEAUTIFUL BURRITOS

makes 8 burritos

INGREDIENTS

8 6-inch (15-cm) round flour tortillas

FOR THE FILLING

16-ounce (454-g) can refried beans

½ cup chopped white onion

1 tablespoon sour cream

½ teaspoon garlic powder

1 teaspoon chili powder

1 teaspoon ground cumin

½ teaspoon salt

2 cups grated cheese (cheddar, Monterey Jack or Colby-Jack)

FOR THE GARNISHES

salsa or pico de gallo

sour cream

black olives

chopped scallions

TOOLS & EQUIPMENT

cutting board
knife
grater
frying pan
tongs
plate
kitchen towel
mixing bowl
fork
measuring cups
measuring spoons
mixing spoon
9 × 13-inch pan
aluminum foil

1. Preheat the oven to 325 degrees.
2. Set a frying pan on the stove over medium-high heat. Soften the tortillas by warming them for 30 seconds on each side. Turn the tortillas with tongs. After warming

them, put the tortillas on a plate and cover them with a towel until you are ready to fill them.

3. Put the beans in a mixing bowl and mash them with a fork until they're smooth. Add the rest of the filling ingredients except the cheese and mix until they're well blended.
4. Put ¼ cup of the bean mixture in the center of a tortilla. Sprinkle ¼ cup of cheese on top of the beans.
5. Fold in one side of the tortilla by 1 inch (2.5 cm).
6. Fold the side of the tortilla closest to you over the middle. Be sure the folded edge stays inside.
7. Roll the tortilla over to make a burrito.
8. Put the burritos in a pan. Cover them with aluminum foil and bake for 20 minutes. Serve the burritos with garnishes.

ENCHILADAS SUPREMAS

makes 8 enchiladas

INGREDIENTS

8 corn tortillas
5 cups grated cheddar cheese

FOR THE SAUCE

1 tablespoon corn oil
1 cup minced white onion
1 clove garlic, minced
28-ounce (794-g) can tomato puree
1 cup water
2 tablespoons chili powder
½ teaspoon ground cumin
½ teaspoon dried oregano
½ teaspoon salt

FOR THE GARNISHES

1 bunch scallions, chopped
sour cream

TO MAKE THE SAUCE

1. Heat the oil in a medium saucepan and add the onion and garlic. Cook over medium heat for about 5 minutes. Stir occasionally with a mixing spoon.
2. Add the tomato puree, water, and spices. Mix until everything is well blended.
3. Turn the heat to medium low. Cover the saucepan and cook for 20 minutes. Stir often with a mixing spoon.
4. Remove the pan from the heat.

TO BUILD THE ENCHILADAS

1. Preheat the oven to 350 degrees.

2. Set a frying pan on the stove over medium-high heat. Soften the tortillas by warming them for 30 seconds on each side. Turn the tortilla with tongs. After warming them, put the tortillas on a plate and cover them with a towel until you are ready to fill them.
3. Using the tongs, dip one tortilla into the sauce mixture. Make sure it is well coated.
4. Put the tortilla on the cutting board and put ½ cup of cheese in the middle.
5. Roll the tortilla to close it and place it seam down in the baking pan.
6. Repeat steps 2 through 4 with the rest of the tortillas.
7. Pour the remaining sauce evenly over all the enchiladas in the baking pan.
8. Bake uncovered in the oven for 15 minutes. Remove the pan from the oven and sprinkle the remaining cup of cheese over the top.
9. Return the pan to the oven for 5 more minutes.
10. Sprinkle chopped scallions over the top and serve with sour cream on the side.

TOOLS & EQUIPMENT

knife
cutting board
grater
measuring spoons
measuring cups
saucepan with lid
mixing spoon
frying pan
tongs
plate
kitchen towel
9 × 13-inch pan

SUPER-DUPER SUBS

makes 8 sandwiches

INGREDIENTS

- 1 loaf soft French bread, about 18 inches (46 cm) long
- ¼ cup mayonnaise
- ½ pound (0.23 kg) provolone cheese, sliced
- ½ pound (0.23 kg) roast turkey, sliced
- ¼ pound (0.11 kg) salami, sliced
- ¼ pound ham (0.11 kg), sliced
- 2 medium tomatoes, sliced ½ inch (1.3 cm) thick
- 5 leaves of leaf lettuce
- 1 green pepper, sliced into rings
- ½ small red onion, sliced thin

1. Use a serrated knife to slice the bread along the long side. Don't cut all the way through to the other side. The bread should open like a book.
2. Spread the mayonnaise along one surface of the bread.
3. Place the cheese along the other surface. Layer each meat evenly on top of the mayonnaise.
4. Place layers of vegetables on top of the meat.
5. Close the sandwich carefully and wrap it in plastic wrap. Put it in the refrigerator for at least an hour.
6. Remove the plastic wrap when you are ready to serve the sandwich. Put 8 toothpicks through the sandwich at even intervals. Then slice between the toothpicks with a serrated knife.

TOOLS & EQUIPMENT

knife
cutting board
serrated knife
silicone spatula
measuring cup
plastic wrap
toothpicks

SLOPPIEST JOES

makes 4 or 6 sandwiches

INGREDIENTS

- 1 pound (0.45 kg) ground beef or ground turkey
- 1 cup chopped onion
- 1 cup ketchup
- 2 tablespoons mustard
- ⅓ cup water
- 2 teaspoons Worcestershire sauce
- ½ teaspoon salt
- 4 large or 6 small hamburger buns
- pickles
- chips

1. Cook the meat and onion in the skillet over medium-high heat. Break up the meat with a mixing spoon so it cooks evenly. When all traces of pink are gone from the meat, have an adult helper drain the grease from the pan.
2. Add the ketchup, mustard, water, Worcestershire sauce, and salt to the skillet. Stir to blend.
3. Cook over low heat for 10 minutes, stirring occasionally.
4. Fill 6 small hamburger buns or 4 large ones with the meat mixture. Serve the sandwiches with pickles, chips, and plenty of napkins!

TOOLS & EQUIPMENT

knife
cutting board
measuring cups
skillet
mixing spoon
measuring spoons
napkins

PHILLY CHEESESTEAK SANDWICH

makes 4 servings

INGREDIENTS

1 tablespoon olive oil

1 teaspoon minced garlic

1 onion, sliced

½ cup sliced green pepper

½ cup sliced mushrooms

½ pound (0.23 kg) rib-eye steak, thinly sliced

2 hoagie buns, cut lengthwise

1 can processed cheddar cheese

salt and pepper

1. Put the oil, garlic, onion, green pepper, and mushrooms in a frying pan. Cook over medium-high heat for 6 minutes. Stir constantly. Remove the pan from the heat. Put the vegetables in a mixing bowl and set the bowl aside.
2. Place the frying pan back on the stove. Put the steak in it and cook over medium-high heat. When the steak begins to turn brown, flip it over with tongs. When both sides are brown, add the vegetables.
3. Stir and cook for 2 minutes. Turn off the stove. Use tongs to put some of the steak and vegetable mixture in each hoagie bun.
4. Add cheese to each sandwich. Let the cheese melt for 1 minute. Season with salt and pepper. Cut each sandwich in half. Enjoy this Philadelphia favorite!

TOOLS & EQUIPMENT

knife
cutting board
measuring spoons
measuring cups
frying pan
mixing spoon
mixing bowl
tongs

SWEET HOME SPICY BBQ

makes 4 servings

INGREDIENTS

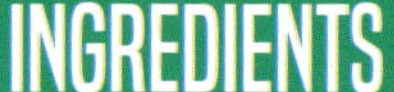

- 4 boneless, skinless chicken breast halves
- 1½ tablespoons sugar
- ½ tablespoon paprika
- ½ teaspoon salt
- ½ teaspoon dry mustard
- ¼ teaspoon chili powder
- ⅛ cup cider vinegar
- ⅛ teaspoon cayenne pepper
- 1 tablespoon Worcestershire sauce
- ¾ cup tomato-vegetable juice
- ¼ cup ketchup
- 1 clove garlic, minced
- 1 tablespoon water

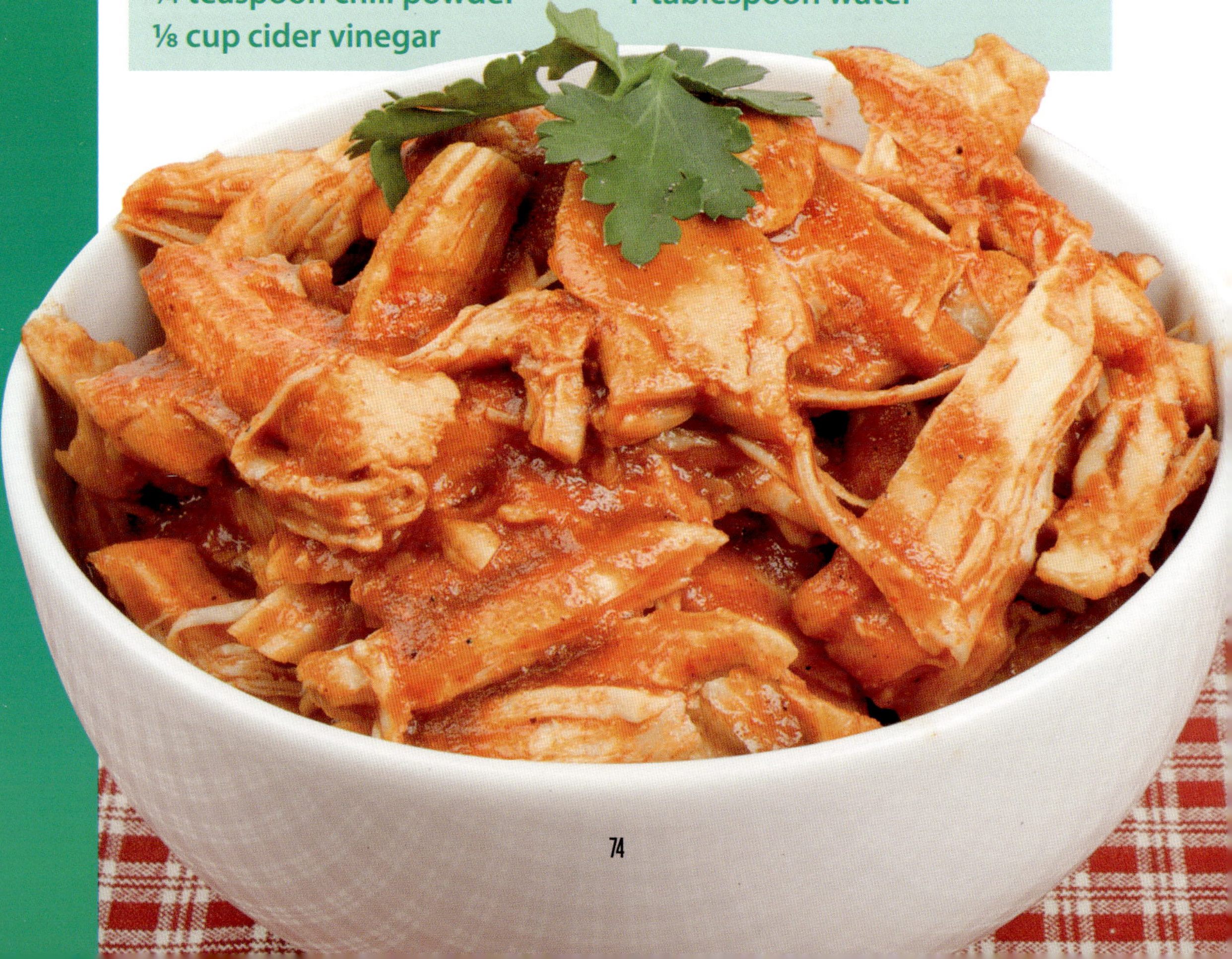

1. Preheat the oven to 350 degrees.
2. Arrange the chicken in the baking dish.
3. Put the remaining ingredients in the mixing bowl. Stir until completely mixed.
4. Pour the mixture over the chicken. Bake for 35 minutes.
5. Take the chicken out of the oven. Use a fork and tongs to shred the chicken breasts. Put the chicken back in the baking dish.
6. Stir to coat the shredded chicken with sauce. Bake another 10 minutes. Take it out and let it cool.

TOOLS & EQUIPMENT

knife
cutting board
9 × 13-inch baking dish
measuring cups
measuring spoons
mixing bowl
mixing spoon
fork
tongs

FRIED RAVIOLI PASTA

makes 6 servings

INGREDIENTS

1 egg
2 tablespoons milk
1 cup breadcrumbs
½ tablespoon oregano
½ tablespoon parsley
½ teaspoon salt
12.5-ounce (354-g) package cheese ravioli
3 cups vegetable oil
1 tablespoon grated Parmesan cheese
16 ounces (454 g) spaghetti sauce

1. Whisk the egg and milk together in a small mixing bowl. Put the breadcrumbs, oregano, parsley, and salt in a separate mixing bowl. Stir.
2. Dip each ravioli in the egg mixture. Then coat it with the breadcrumb mixture.
3. Put the oil in a frying pan. Heat over medium heat. Use tongs to carefully put the ravioli in the oil. Fry 1 minute. Use a slotted spoon to flip the ravioli. Fry the other side for 1 minute.

4. Place the ravioli on paper towels. Pat them to remove extra oil. Top them with cheese.
5. Put the spaghetti sauce in a saucepan. Bring it to a boil and then turn off the heat. Pour the sauce into a serving bowl. Serve as a dip for the ravioli!

TOOLS & EQUIPMENT

grater
mixing bowls
measuring spoons
whisk
measuring cups
mixing spoon
frying pan
tongs
slotted spoon
paper towels
saucepan
serving bowl

YUMMY CLASSIC MEATLOAF

makes 8 servings

INGREDIENTS

- non-stick cooking spray
- butter crackers
- ½ onion, chopped
- 2 tablespoons butter
- 2 teaspoons minced garlic
- 1½ pounds (0.68 kg) ground beef
- 1 egg
- 1 cup milk
- 2 tablespoons brown sugar
- ⅔ cup ketchup
- 1½ tablespoons mustard
- 1 tablespoon Worcestershire sauce
- 1 teaspoon salt
- ½ teaspoon pepper

1. Preheat the oven to 350 degrees. Grease the loaf pan with non-stick cooking spray. Fill a plastic bag with crackers. Crush them with a rolling pin. Measure 1 cup of crumbs.
2. Put the onion, butter, and garlic in the saucepan. Cook over medium heat for 5 minutes. Take the pan off the heat.
3. Put the onion mixture, ground beef, egg, milk, and cracker crumbs in a large mixing bowl. Stir well. Spoon the mixture into the loaf pan.
4. Put the brown sugar, ketchup, mustard, Worcestershire sauce, salt, and pepper in a small mixing bowl. Whisk together. Spread the mixture on top of the meatloaf. Bake for 1 hour and 45 minutes.

TOOLS & EQUIPMENT

knife
cutting board
9 × 5-inch loaf pan
plastic zipper bag
rolling pin
measuring cups
measuring spoons
saucepan
mixing spoon
mixing bowls
whisk
silicone spatula

SENSATIONAL SESAME NOODLES

makes 4 servings

INGREDIENTS

- 8 ounces (227 g) angel hair pasta
- 3 tablespoons sesame seeds
- ¼ cup peanut butter
- ¼ cup water
- 3 tablespoons soy sauce
- 2 tablespoons sesame oil
- 1 tablespoon brown sugar
- 1 tablespoon rice vinegar
- 2 cloves garlic, minced
- ¼ teaspoon white pepper
- 2 scallions, chopped
- ½ red pepper, diced
- 1 cup fresh mung bean sprouts
- ¼ cup peanuts, chopped

1. Preheat the oven to 275 degrees.
2. Cook the pasta according to the package's instructions. Rinse the cooked pasta with cold water. Stir to separate the strands. Leave it in the strainer to drain.
3. Spread the sesame seeds on a baking sheet. Put them in the oven for 5 minutes. The seeds will turn a light golden brown.
4. Put the peanut butter, water, soy sauce, oil, brown sugar, vinegar, garlic, white pepper, and sesame seeds in a blender. Blend until smooth.
5. Put the drained pasta in a large bowl. Pour the blended ingredients over it. Stir gently with a mixing spoon until the pasta is evenly coated with the dressing. Divide the pasta into four bowls.
6. Garnish each bowl with scallions, red pepper, bean sprouts, and peanuts.

TOOLS & EQUIPMENT

knife
cutting board
large saucepan
strainer
baking sheet
measuring cups
measuring spoons
blender
mixing bowl
mixing spoon
4 dinner bowls

SPECTACULAR SUKIYAKI

makes 4 to 6 servings

INGREDIENTS

- 1 cup water
- ½ cup soy sauce
- ½ cup mirin
- 2 tablespoons sugar
- 1 package of ready-to-eat shirataki noodles
- 3 tablespoons canola oil
- 1 pound (0.45 kg) lean beef steak, cut into thin strips
- 1 large yellow onion sliced into moon shapes
- 3 carrots, peeled and sliced into thin slices on the diagonal
- 8 mushrooms, cut in half
- 14-ounce (397-g) package firm tofu, cut into 1-inch (2.5-cm) cubes
- 6 scallions, sliced into 1-inch (2.5-cm) pieces
- rice, cooked

TOOLS & EQUIPMENT

- knife
- cutting board
- peeler
- measuring cups
- measuring spoons
- saucepan
- mixing spoon
- strainer
- mixing bowl
- kitchen scissors
- large, heavy-bottomed pot
- tongs
- large serving bowls

1. Put the water, soy sauce, mirin, and sugar in a small saucepan. Cook over high heat. Stir with a mixing spoon until the sugar dissolves. When the mixture boils, remove it from the heat and let it cool. This is the sauce.
2. Drain the shirataki noodles. Put the noodles in a bowl. Cut them into

several pieces with clean kitchen scissors. Set this bowl aside.

3. Make sure the prepared vegetables are handy. You will need to add them to the pot quickly. Put the oil in a large, heavy-bottomed pot. Heat over medium-high heat.
4. Add the beef. Sauté for 2 minutes. Use tongs to turn the meat. Move the meat to one side of the pan.
5. Add the onions and carrots. Keep each ingredient in its own part of the pot. Sauté for 3 minutes.
6. Add the mushrooms. Stir the vegetables to keep them from sticking to the bottom of the pot. Add the sauce and bring to a boil.
7. Add the shirataki noodles, tofu, and scallions to the pot. Cook until the meat is no longer pink and the vegetables are hot. The total cooking time should be about 10 minutes. Serve in large bowls with steamed rice on the side.

CASHEW CHICKEN STIR FRY

makes 4 servings

INGREDIENTS

- 2 tablespoons oyster sauce
- 1 tablespoon soy sauce
- ⅛ teaspoon white pepper
- 2 teaspoons sesame oil
- water
- 1 boneless skinless chicken breast
- 2 tablespoons cornstarch
- 2 tablespoons canola oil
- 1 bunch scallions, cut into 1-inch (2.5-cm) slices
- 1 green pepper, cleaned and cut into thin strips
- 6 thin slices peeled ginger root
- ½ cup cashews
- white rice, cooked

TOOLS & EQUIPMENT

- knife
- cutting board
- peeler
- measuring spoons
- measuring cups
- mixing bowls
- whisk
- paper towels
- mixing spoon
- wok or large frying pan

1. Put the oyster sauce, soy sauce, white pepper, 1 teaspoon sesame oil, and ¼ cup water in a mixing bowl. Whisk well.
2. Pat the chicken dry using paper towels. Cut the chicken into cubes.
3. Put the cornstarch, 2 teaspoons water, and 1 teaspoon sesame oil in a large bowl. Whisk until smooth.
4. Add the chicken pieces. Mix well to coat the chicken. Marinate the chicken for 15 minutes.
5. Heat the canola oil in a large frying pan or wok over medium high heat. Use a mixing spoon to remove the chicken from the marinade. Put the chicken in the pan. Sauté for 10 minutes.
6. Add the scallions, green pepper, and ginger. Sauté for 5 minutes.
7. Add the cashews and oyster sauce mixture. Stir to coat all the ingredients with the sauce. Cook for 5 minutes, stirring often. The sauce will thicken a little bit as it cooks.
8. Test one piece of chicken to be sure it is cooked in the middle. If there is no pink color, the chicken is done. Serve over steamed white rice.

CLASSIC CROQUE MONSIEUR

makes 2 sandwiches

INGREDIENTS

4 slices of deli ham
½ cup grated Swiss cheese
4 slices bread
2 eggs
1 tablespoon half-and-half
2 tablespoons butter

1. Put two slices of ham and half of the cheese between two slices of bread. Put the remaining ham and cheese between the other two slices of bread.
2. Whisk together the eggs and half-and-half in a mixing bowl.
3. Dip each side of the sandwiches in the egg mixture.
4. Melt the butter in a frying pan. Fry the sandwiches over low heat until they are golden brown on the bottom.
5. Use a spatula to flip the sandwiches over. Cook until the other side is golden brown and the cheese is melted.

TOOLS & EQUIPMENT

grater
measuring cup
measuring spoon
whisk
mixing bowl
frying pan
spatula

SAVORY ROAST CHICKEN

makes 4 to 6 servings

INGREDIENTS

- 1 whole chicken, between 3 and 4 pounds (1.4 and 1.8 kg)
- 4 teaspoons kosher salt
- ¼ teaspoon pepper

1. Preheat the oven to 450 degrees.
2. Pat the chicken dry with paper towels.
3. Sprinkle 1 teaspoon kosher salt and the pepper inside the chicken. Cross the ends of the legs. Tie them together with a piece of kitchen string.
4. Put the chicken on the baking sheet with the breast side up. Sprinkle 3 teaspoons kosher salt over the chicken.
5. Put the chicken in the oven for 1 hour. Have an adult helper use a meat thermometer to see if the chicken is done. Insert it between the leg and thigh but not touching a bone. When the thermometer reads 165 degrees the chicken is done. Take the chicken out of the oven and let it sit for 15 minutes. Have an adult helper cut the chicken into pieces.

TOOLS & EQUIPMENT

paper towels
cutting board
measuring spoons
kitchen string
baking sheet
meat thermometer
knife

FANTASTIC FETTUCCINE ALFREDO

makes 4 servings

INGREDIENTS

salt
2 tablespoons butter
1 large shallot, minced
2 cups heavy whipping cream
½ cup grated Parmesan cheese
¼ teaspoon pepper
⅛ teaspoon nutmeg
8 ounces (227 g) fettuccine noodles
¼ cup chopped Italian parsley

TOOLS & EQUIPMENT

knife
cutting board
grater
heavy-bottomed pot with lid
measuring spoons
mixing spoon
saucepan
measuring cups
strainer
serving bowl

1. Put 4 quarts of water in a large heavy-bottomed pot. Add 1 tablespoon of salt. Stir to dissolve the salt. Cover the pot and bring the water to a boil.
2. Meanwhile, heat the butter in a medium saucepan over medium-high heat.
3. When the butter is melted, add the shallot. Sauté over medium heat for 3 minutes, stirring with a mixing spoon.
4. Turn down the heat. Stir in the cream, cheese, ¼ teaspoon salt, pepper, and nutmeg. Cook over low heat for 5 minutes, stirring often.
5. Add the fettuccine noodles to the boiling water. The package will tell you how long to boil the noodles.
6. While the fettuccine cooks, continue cooking the sauce over low heat, stirring often.
7. Drain the fettuccine in a strainer. Then put it in a large serving bowl. Pour the sauce over the fettuccine. Stir to coat the pasta with the sauce. Let stand for 5 minutes.
8. Sprinkle with parsley and serve.

LEGENDARY LASAGNA

makes about 8 servings

INGREDIENTS

3 cups ricotta cheese
2 eggs
1 cup Parmesan cheese, grated
¼ cup Italian parsley, chopped
4 cups jarred red sauce
9-ounce (255-g) package no-boil lasagna noodles
8 ounces (227 g) mozzarella cheese, grated
olive oil

TOOLS & EQUIPMENT

knife
cutting board
grater
measuring cups
mixing bowl
mixing spoon
9 × 9-inch baking dish
silicone spatula
aluminum foil

1. Preheat the oven to 350 degrees.
2. Put the ricotta cheese, eggs, Parmesan cheese, and parsley in a mixing bowl. Mix with a mixing spoon.
3. Spread 1 cup of red sauce evenly over the bottom of the baking dish. Cover the red sauce with a layer of noodles.
4. Spread half the cheese mixture over the noodles. Spread 1 cup of sauce over the cheese mixture.
5. Cover the sauce with a second layer of noodles. Spread the rest of the cheese mixture over the noodles.
6. Spread 1 cup of red sauce over the cheese mixture. Cover the red sauce with a third layer of noodles. Spread 1 cup of red sauce over the noodles. Sprinkle the mozzarella cheese evenly over the top.
7. Cut a piece of aluminum foil large enough to cover the dish. Rub oil on one side. Put the foil oil side down over the dish. Press it tightly around the edges. Bake covered for 45 minutes.
8. Remove the foil. Continue baking for 15 more minutes. It should be bubbly around the edges. Have an adult helper test the center to make sure it is hot all the way through. Remove the lasagna from the oven. Let it stand for 10 minutes before serving.

GREEK HERBED CHICKEN

makes 4 to 6 servings

INGREDIENTS

- ⅓ cup lemon juice
- ⅔ cup olive oil
- 4 cloves garlic, minced
- ¼ cup chopped fresh oregano
- 2 tablespoons chopped fresh parsley
- 1 teaspoon salt
- ½ teaspoon pepper
- 1 pound (0.45 kg) chicken breasts, cut into serving pieces

1. Put the lemon juice, oil, and garlic in a small bowl. Whisk them together. Add the oregano, parsley, salt, and pepper and mix. This is the marinade.
2. Put the chicken pieces in a large bowl. Pour the marinade over chicken. Mix to coat the chicken evenly with the marinade. Cover the bowl with plastic wrap. Refrigerate for at least two hours and up to 24 hours.
3. Preheat the oven to 400 degrees.
4. Put the marinated chicken into a baking dish. Bake for 30 minutes.
5. Turn the oven down to 350 degrees. Bake for 30 to 45 minutes until chicken is cooked through. To check whether the chicken is done, cut into a thick piece. If it is not pink inside, the chicken is done.

TOOLS & EQUIPMENT

knife
cutting board
juicer
measuring cups
mixing bowls
whisk
measuring spoons
mixing spoon
plastic wrap
9 × 9-inch baking dish

SALADS & SIDES

Any good homemade meal needs delicious extras. Make homemade salads and side dishes! They make any meal complete.

Wonderful Wild Rice Pilaf

Creole Cooked Okra & Tomatoes

Superb Salad Niçoise

Golden State Potato Salad
Green Beans with Almonds
Seasoned Chickpea Salad

GOLDEN STATE POTATO SALAD

makes 4 servings

INGREDIENTS

5 red potatoes
1 tablespoon salt
½ cup grated Parmesan cheese
3 cloves garlic, minced
¼ cup chopped parsley
¼ cup olive oil
1 tablespoon Dijon mustard
2 tablespoons rice vinegar
3 tablespoons mayonnaise
1 teaspoon pepper
3 scallions, chopped

1. Cut the potatoes into small pieces.
2. Put the potatoes in a saucepan and cover with water. Add the salt. Bring to a boil, then reduce the heat to low. Cover and cook until you can easily pierce the potatoes with a fork. It takes about 15 minutes.
3. Drain the potatoes. Let them cool completely.
4. Put the cheese, garlic, parsley, oil, mustard, vinegar, mayonnaise, and pepper in a mixing bowl. Stir.
5. Add the potatoes and scallions to the cheese mixture. Toss to coat. Chow down on this California classic!

TOOLS & EQUIPMENT

knife	**fork**
cutting board	**strainer**
grater	**measuring cups**
measuring spoons	**mixing bowl**
saucepan with lid	**mixing spoon**

SEASONED CHICKPEA SALAD

makes 6 to 8 servings

INGREDIENTS

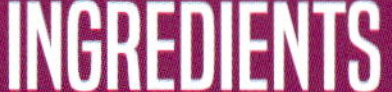

- 4 tablespoons olive oil
- 1 tablespoon red wine vinegar
- 1 tablespoon lemon juice
- ¾ cup finely chopped parsley
- ½ teaspoon salt
- ¼ teaspoon pepper
- 2 15-ounce (425-g) cans chickpeas, rinsed and drained
- 1 white onion about 3 inches (7.6 cm) across, minced
- 4 scallions, chopped

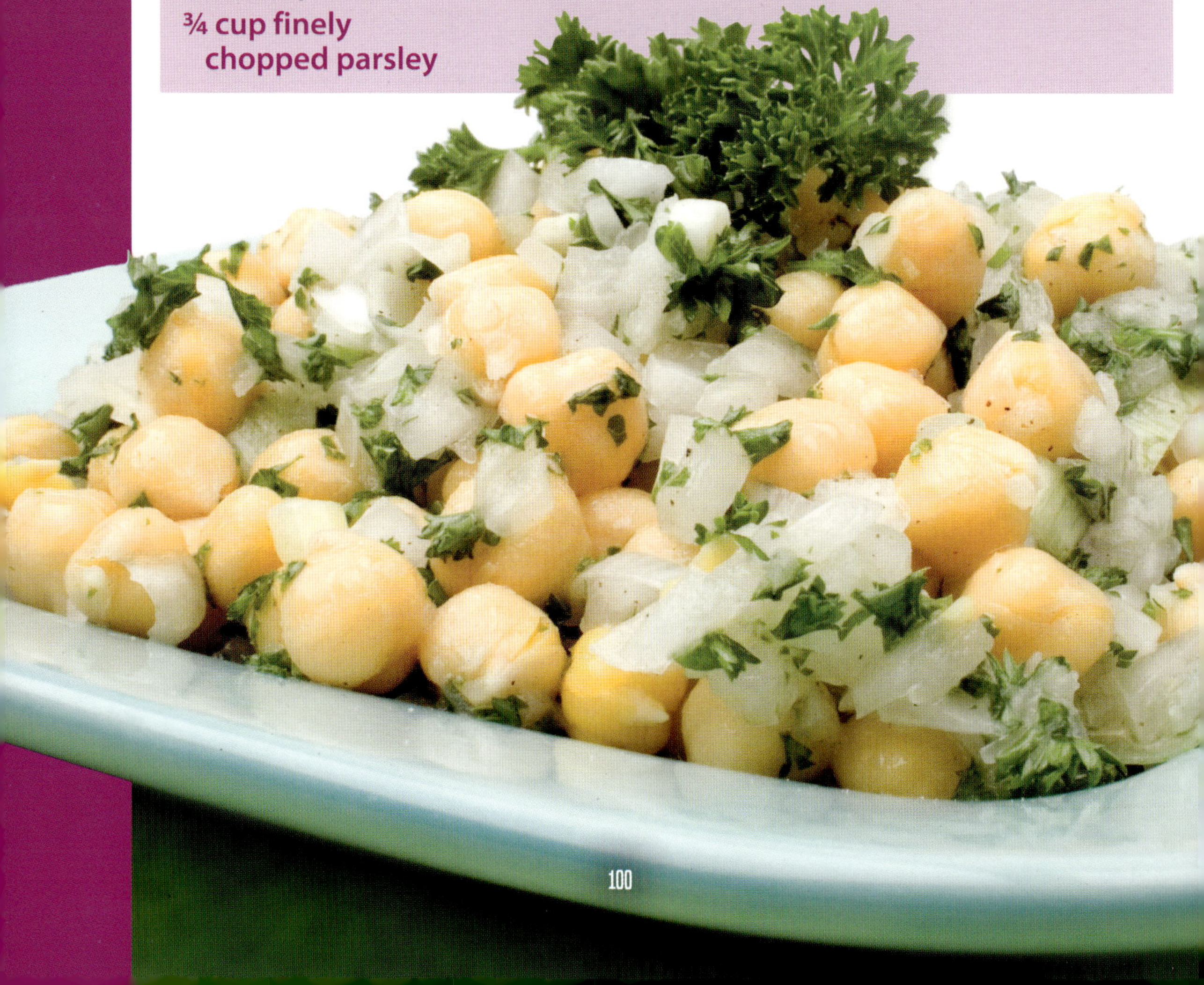

1. Put the oil, vinegar, and lemon juice in a large bowl. Whisk them together.
2. Add the parsley, salt, and pepper. Whisk to blend.
3. Add the chickpeas, onion, and scallions. Mix well with a mixing spoon.
4. Chill for at least 1 hour before serving.

TOOLS & EQUIPMENT

knife
cutting board
juicer
measuring spoons
mixing bowl
whisk
measuring cups
mixing spoon

TRY THIS

Use ½ cup finely chopped cilantro instead of the parsley. Also add 1 teaspoon ground cumin.

SUPERB SALAD NIÇOISE

makes 4 large salads

INGREDIENTS

- ½ pound (0.23 kg) fresh green beans, ends trimmed
- 4 small red potatoes
- 2 tablespoons red wine vinegar
- 5–6 tablespoons olive oil
- ¼ teaspoon salt
- ½ teaspoon pepper
- 2 tablespoons chopped fresh herbs (oregano, parsley, dill, thyme, or a combination)
- 1 head romaine lettuce, washed and dried
- 4 plum tomatoes, sliced
- 4 hard-boiled eggs, peeled and sliced
- 6-ounce (170-g) can tuna, rinsed and drained in a strainer
- 20 black olives

1. Fill a saucepan with water and bring to a boil. Add the beans and boil for 5 minutes. Drain them in a strainer and rinse with cold water. Refrigerate the beans until you are ready to use them.
2. Put the potatoes in a medium saucepan and cover them with water. Bring to a boil, then reduce the heat to low. Simmer the potatoes for 15 minutes. Then check them for doneness. A fork should go through the potato easily. If the potatoes are still too firm, continue simmering until the fork goes through easily.
3. Use a strainer to drain the potatoes. Rinse with cold water. Chill for at least 1 hour in the refrigerator. Then cut them into slices.
4. Put the vinegar, oil, salt, pepper, and herbs in a small jar with a tight-fitting lid. Shake until the ingredients are well blended. This is the dressing.
5. Divide the lettuce evenly between four dinner plates. Spread the lettuce leaves around each plate.
6. Arrange the potatoes, tomatoes, beans, eggs, tuna, and olives evenly over each plate of lettuce. Pour some of the dressing on each salad and serve.

TOOLS & EQUIPMENT

knife
cutting board
peeler
strainer
measuring cup
saucepans with lids
fork
measuring spoons
small jar with lid
4 dinner plates

SALADS & SIDES

CRISPY CRUNCHY VEGGIE SALAD

makes 6 to 8 servings

INGREDIENTS

2 large tomatoes, each sliced into 8 wedges

1 cucumber peeled, seeded, and cubed into ½-inch (1.3-cm) pieces

6 radishes, sliced thin

6 to 8 scallions, sliced thin

1 green pepper, cut into ¾-inch (1.9-cm) squares

2 carrots, sliced into ¼-inch (0.6-cm) slices

¼ cup olive oil

2 tablespoons lemon juice

¼ cup chopped fresh parsley

½ teaspoon salt

whole peppercorns

1. Put the tomatoes and all the vegetables in a mixing bowl. Set this bowl aside.
2. Whisk together the oil and lemon juice in a small bowl to make the dressing.
3. Pour the dressing over the vegetables. Use two forks to toss the salad.
4. Add parsley and mix well.
5. Grind pepper over the top, then mix to blend.
6. Add salt and pepper to taste. Chill for at least 1 hour before serving.

TRY THIS

To peel and seed a cucumber, remove the peel with a vegetable peeler. Cut the cucumber in half the long way. Then use a spoon to scrape away the seeds.

TOOLS & EQUIPMENT

knife
cutting board
peeler
spoon
juicer
measuring cups
measuring spoons
mixing bowls
whisk
forks
pepper grinder

CLASSIC MACARONI SALAD

makes 4 cups

INGREDIENTS

- 16 ounces (454 g) elbow macaroni
- 1 tablespoon olive oil
- 1 small onion, finely chopped
- 2 stalks celery, finely chopped
- 1 cup mayonnaise
- 3 tablespoons white vinegar
- 1 tablespoon yellow mustard
- 1 teaspoon salt
- ½ teaspoon pepper
- 4 hard-boiled eggs, peeled and chopped
- 3 tablespoons chopped fresh parsley or chives
- salt and pepper
- paprika (optional)

1. Cook the macaroni according to directions on the package. Drain and rinse the macaroni. Shake the strainer to remove excess water. Put the macaroni in a large mixing bowl. Add the oil and toss to coat. Let the macaroni cool.
2. Add the onion and celery. Mix well.
3. Whisk the mayonnaise, vinegar, mustard, salt, and pepper together in a small mixing bowl. Pour it over the macaroni and vegetables. Mix well. Make sure everything is well coated.
4. Gently stir in the eggs and herbs. Add salt and pepper to taste. Cover the bowl with plastic wrap and refrigerate for at least 3 hours before serving. Just before serving, mix it again. Sprinkle paprika on top if you like.

TOOLS & EQUIPMENT

knife
cutting board
saucepans with lids
strainer
mixing bowls
measuring spoons
mixing spoon
measuring cups
whisk
plastic wrap

CHIPOTLE CHICKEN SALAD

makes 6 servings

- olive oil
- 1 pound (0.45 kg) chicken breasts
- 1 large red onion, cut in half, then sliced
- 1 cup mayonnaise
- juice and zest from 1 small lime
- 2 teaspoons adobo sauce (from canned chipotles)
- 2 cloves garlic, minced
- salt and pepper
- buns or lettuce

1. Preheat the oven to 375 degrees. Lightly grease a baking sheet with oil.
2. Pat the chicken breasts dry with paper towels. Put the chicken on the baking sheet. Put the onion slices around the chicken. Drizzle oil over the chicken and onions.
3. Bake the chicken and onions for 30 minutes. Remove it from the oven and let it cool.
4. Whisk together the mayonnaise, lime juice and zest, adobo sauce, and garlic in a mixing bowl.
5. Cube the chicken and add it to the mayonnaise mixture. Add the onions and mix until everything is well coated. Add salt and pepper to taste.
6. Serve on buns for sandwiches, or on lettuce for salads.

TRY THIS

For a lower fat version, substitute Greek yogurt for some or all of the mayonnaise.

TOOLS & EQUIPMENT

knife
cutting board
grater or zester
juicer
baking sheet
paper towels
measuring cups
measuring spoons
mixing bowl
whisk
mixing spoon

BY THE SEA BEANS & RICE

makes 6 servings

INGREDIENTS

¼ cup vegetable oil
1 cup chopped onion
1 green pepper, chopped
2 garlic cloves, minced
9 cups water
15.25-ounce (432-g) can kidney beans
1 teaspoon salt
1 teaspoon cayenne pepper
2 teaspoons dried oregano
2 turkey sausages, sliced
1½ cup white rice

1. Heat the oil in a large saucepan for 30 seconds. Stir in the onion, green pepper, and garlic.
2. Cook for 5 minutes on medium heat, or until the onions turn clear.
3. Add 6 cups water and the beans. Add the salt, cayenne pepper, and oregano. Stir everything together. Cover the pan. Cook on medium-low heat for 2 hours.
4. Stir in the sausages. Put the lid back on and cook for another 30 minutes.
5. Put the rice and 3 cups water in a medium saucepan. Bring the water to a boil. Turn down the heat. Let it simmer for 20 minutes. Serve the beans over the rice.

TOOLS & EQUIPMENT

knife
cutting board
measuring cups
saucepans with lids
mixing spoon
measuring spoons

CREOLE COOKED OKRA & TOMATOES

makes 5 servings

INGREDIENTS

3 cups chopped okra
1 cup chopped onion
1 cup chopped red pepper
¾ cup canned tomatoes, chopped
5 tablespoons vegetable oil
1 teaspoon basil
1 teaspoon chopped scallions
1½ tablespoons salt
¼ teaspoon cayenne pepper
¼ teaspoon black pepper
½ teaspoon dried thyme
½ teaspoon dried oregano
1 tablespoon minced garlic

1. Preheat the oven to 300 degrees.
2. Put all ingredients in a large mixing bowl. Stir well. Make sure the okra gets coated with the oil and seasonings.
3. Put the mixture in the baking dish. Cover it with aluminum foil.
4. Bake 90 minutes. Stir the mixture once every 30 minutes while baking.
5. Remove the aluminum foil for the last 15 minutes of baking time. Take the dish out of the oven.

TOOLS & EQUIPMENT

knife
cutting board
measuring cups
measuring spoons
large mixing bowl
mixing spoon
8 × 8-inch baking dish
aluminum foil

WONDERFUL WILD RICE PILAF

makes 8 servings

INGREDIENTS

1 cup walnuts
1 tablespoon olive oil
½ cup chopped onion
½ cup chopped carrots
½ cup peas
½ cup dried cranberries
½ teaspoon salt
4 cups chicken broth
1 cup white rice
¾ cup wild rice

1. Preheat the oven to 350 degrees.
2. Put the walnuts on the baking sheet in a single layer. Bake for 8 minutes. Take them out. After they cool, chop them.
3. Put the oil in a small frying pan. Heat over medium heat for 1 minute. Add the onion, carrots, peas, cranberries, and salt. Stir and cook 5 minutes. Remove the pan from heat and let it cool.
4. Put the broth, white rice, and wild rice in a large saucepan. Bring to a boil over high heat.
5. Turn the heat to low. Cover the pan. Cook for 40 minutes.
6. Stir the chopped walnuts and cooked vegetables into the rice mixture.

TOOLS & EQUIPMENT

knife
cutting board
measuring cups
baking sheet
measuring spoons
frying pan
mixing spoon
saucepan with lid

SOUTHERN BAKED BISCUITS

makes 36 biscuits

INGREDIENTS

- 2½ teaspoons baking powder
- ½ teaspoon baking soda
- ½ teaspoon salt
- 1 tablespoon sugar
- 2¼ cups flour
- ½ cup butter
- ¾ cup buttermilk

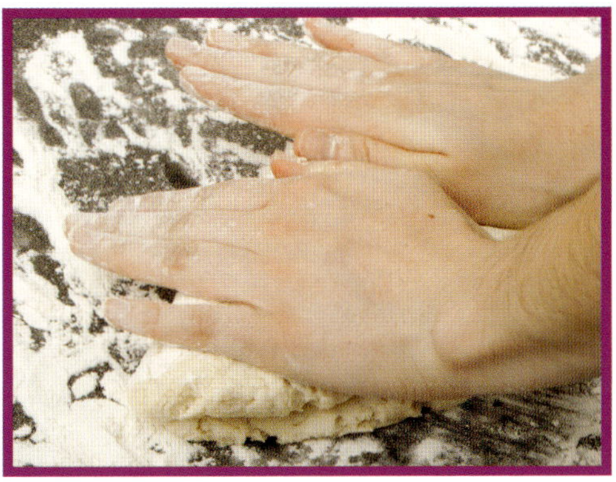

1. Preheat the oven to 400 degrees.
2. Put the baking powder, baking soda, salt, sugar, and 2 cups flour in a large mixing bowl. Stir.
3. Cut the butter into small chunks. Add it to the mixing bowl. Mix the dough with your hands until it is crumbly. Add the buttermilk. Stir with a mixing spoon until smooth.
4. Spread the remaining flour on a clean, flat surface. Place the dough on top. Knead for 2 minutes.
5. Put the dough on the baking sheet. Shape it into a flat square with 6-inch (15-cm) sides. Cut shallow lines in the dough. Do not cut all the way through. Make 36 equal squares.
6. Bake for 15 minutes. Let the biscuits cool until you can touch them safely. Pull the biscuits apart.

TOOLS & EQUIPMENT

measuring cups
measuring spoons
mixing bowl
mixing spoon
knife
cutting board
baking sheet

FANTASTIC FRY BREAD

makes about 10 pieces

INGREDIENTS

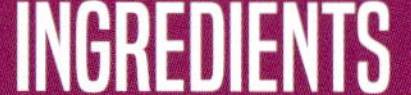

- 3 cups flour
- 1 tablespoon baking powder
- ½ teaspoon salt
- 1 cup warm water
- 2 cups cooking oil
- jam or honey (optional)

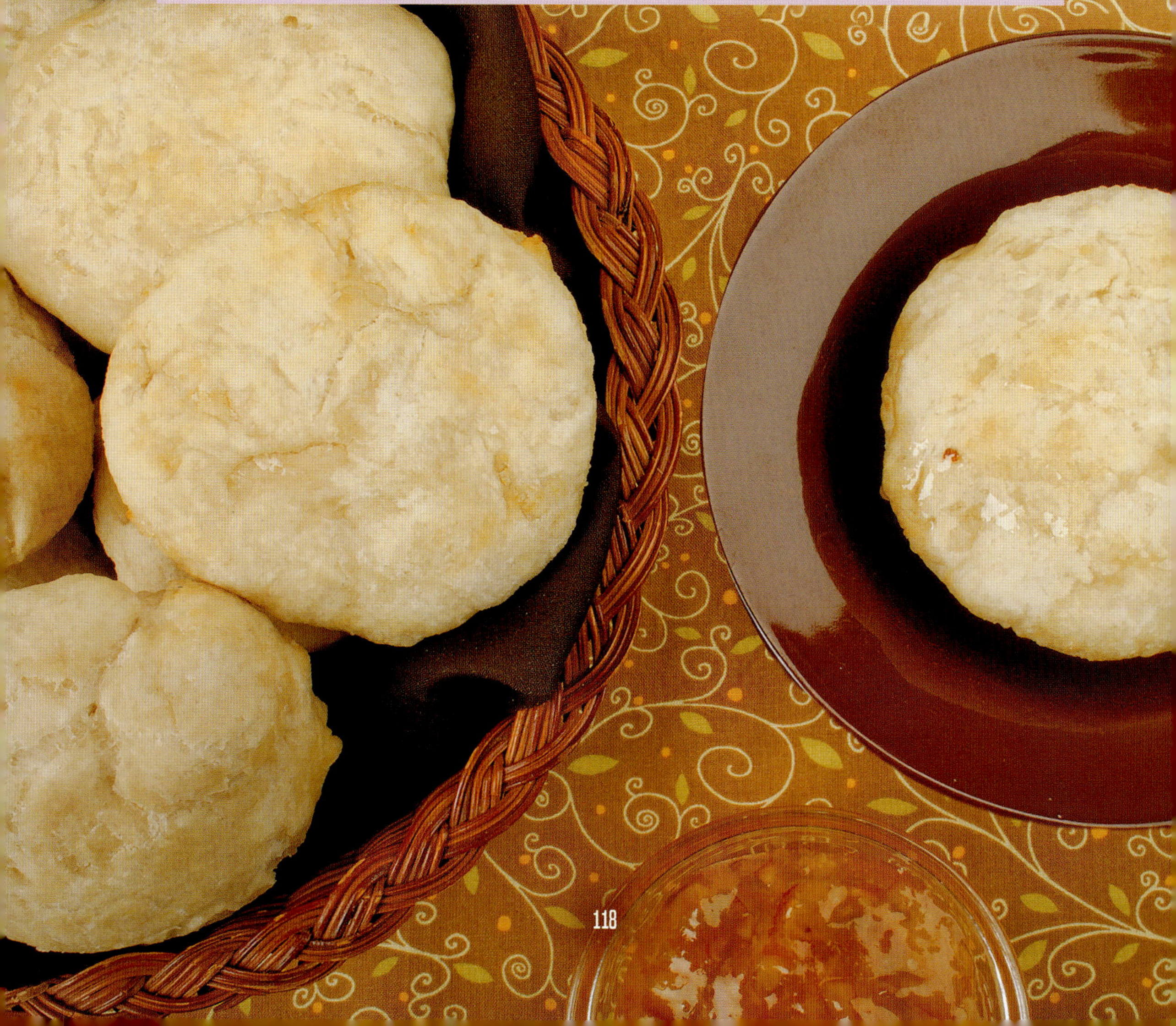

1. Put the flour, baking powder, and salt in a large mixing bowl. Stir.
2. Slowly add ½ cup of warm water. Mix with your hands by squeezing the dough. Add ¾ cups of warm water. Mix with your hands. Squeeze and mix the dough until it is soft. Cover the bowl with plastic wrap. Let it sit for 15 minutes.
3. Roll three tablespoons of dough into a ball. Flatten the ball with your hand. Make it as flat as possible. Repeat until you've used all of the dough.
4. Put the oil in the frying pan. Heat until it is bubbling. Put the dough circles in three at a time. Cook them until bubbles appear on top of the dough. Flip them over with the tongs. Cook for another 30 seconds.
5. Put the fry bread on paper towels to cool. Serve with jam or honey if you like.

TOOLS & EQUIPMENT

measuring cups
measuring spoons
mixing bowl
mixing spoon
plastic wrap
frying pan
tongs
paper towels

CHINESE FRIED RICE

makes 6 to 8 servings

INGREDIENTS

- 2 tablespoons canola oil
- 3 cloves garlic, minced
- 1 cup frozen green peas
- 8 mushrooms, sliced
- 6 cups rice, cooked and cooled
- 3 tablespoons soy sauce
- ⅛ teaspoon white pepper
- 5 scallions, chopped
- 2 eggs, lightly beaten
- 1 cup mung bean sprouts

1. Heat the oil in a wok or a large frying pan.
2. When the oil is hot, add the garlic. Sauté over medium-high heat for 2 minutes.
3. Add the peas and mushrooms. Sauté for 2 minutes.
4. Add the rice and stir well using a mixing spoon.
5. Add in the soy sauce, white pepper, and scallions. Continue to cook and stir for 5 minutes.
6. Make a well in the middle of the rice. Pour the eggs into the well. After about 30 seconds, cover the eggs with the rice.
7. After 1 minute, stir to blend in the eggs. Continue stirring until the eggs are cooked.
8. Add the bean sprouts and stir to mix before serving.

TOOLS & EQUIPMENT

knife
cutting board
mixing bowl
whisk
measuring spoons
wok or frying pan
measuring cups
mixing spoon

AMAZING MEXICAN RICE

makes 8 servings

INGREDIENTS

- 1 cup long-grain white rice
- 2⅓ cups water
- 1 teaspoon salt
- 1 tablespoon olive oil
- 2 carrots, chopped
- 1 small white onion, minced
- 1 clove garlic, minced
- 1 stalk celery, chopped
- 14-ounce (397-g) can diced tomatoes
- 1 teaspoon chili powder

1. Put the rice, 2 cups water, and the salt in a medium saucepan. Bring to a boil over medium-high heat. Stir.
2. Cover the saucepan and turn the heat to low.
3. Let the rice cook over low heat for 18 minutes. Do not remove the lid.
4. Turn off the heat and let the rice sit for 10 minutes. Then take the lid off the pan.
5. Use a fork to separate the grains of rice. Put the rice in a mixing bowl and cover it with a kitchen towel.
6. Wash and dry the saucepan.
7. Heat the oil in the saucepan. Add the carrots, onion, garlic, and celery. Cook over medium heat for 10 minutes, stirring occasionally.
8. Add the diced tomatoes, chili powder, and ⅓ cup water. Cook for 5 minutes, stirring occasionally.
9. Add the rice to the saucepan and stir to blend well. Cook over low heat 1 to 2 minutes, stirring constantly. Serve.

TOOLS & EQUIPMENT

knife
cutting board
saucepan with lid
measuring cups
measuring spoons
mixing spoon
fork
mixing bowl
kitchen towel

CREAMY MASHED POTATOES

makes 8 servings

INGREDIENTS

- 3 pounds (1.4 kg) Yukon Gold potatoes, peeled and cut in half
- 6 tablespoons butter
- 1½ cups whole milk
- salt and pepper

1. Put the potatoes in a large pot. Add cold water until the potatoes are covered. Bring to a boil over high heat. Cook for 10 to 12 minutes until the potatoes are tender but not mushy. Remove from heat and drain the potatoes. Do not rinse them.
2. Put the butter in a microwave-safe bowl. Melt it in the microwave using low power for 30 seconds. Put the milk in another microwave-safe bowl and heat it for 1 minute using high power.
3. Place the hot potatoes in a large mixing bowl. Mash them until most of the lumps are gone.
4. Stir the butter into the potatoes.
5. Stir in half of the warmed milk. Continue adding milk until the mashed potatoes are smooth and creamy. Add salt and pepper to taste.

TRY THIS

For richer mashed potatoes, substitute light or heavy cream for the milk.

TOOLS & EQUIPMENT

peeler
knife
cutting board
pot
strainer
2 microwave-safe bowls
measuring cup
mixing bowl
potato masher
mixing spoon

SWEET GLAZED CARROTS

makes 6 servings

INGREDIENTS

- 4 cups peeled, sliced carrots
- ⅓ cup fresh orange juice
- 1 tablespoon cornstarch
- 2 tablespoons maple syrup
- salt and pepper
- 3 tablespoons chopped fresh parsley

1. Put the carrots in a saucepan with 1 inch (2.5 cm) of water. Bring to a boil. Cover the pan and cook over low heat until the carrots are tender. It takes about 8 minutes. Drain the carrots.
2. Put the orange juice and cornstarch in the saucepan. Whisk until smooth. Add the maple syrup. Bring to a boil. Stir and boil for 1 minute.
3. Return the carrots to the saucepan. Stir and cook over low heat until the carrots are hot. Add salt and pepper to taste.
4. Put the carrots in a serving bowl and sprinkle the chopped parsley on top.

TOOLS & EQUIPMENT

peeler
knife
cutting board
measuring cups
saucepan with lid
strainer
measuring spoons
whisk
mixing spoon
serving bowl

TRY THIS

You can substitute brown sugar for the maple syrup.

GREEN BEANS WITH ALMONDS

makes 6 servings

INGREDIENTS

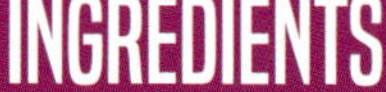

- 1 pound (0.45 kg) fresh green beans, ends trimmed
- 2 tablespoons butter
- 2 tablespoons olive oil
- ½ cup slivered almonds
- salt and pepper

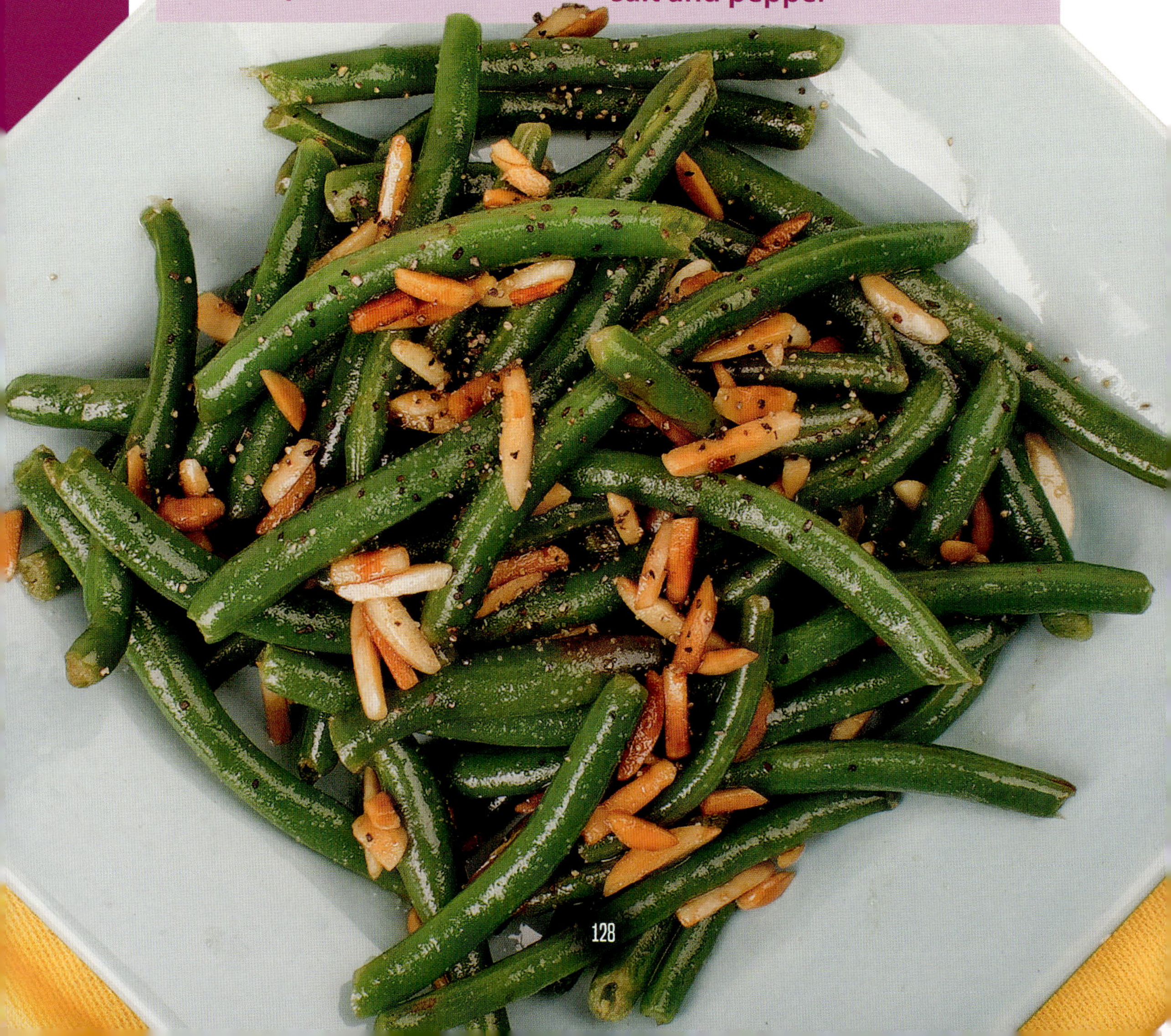

1. Fill a large saucepan halfway with water. Bring it to a boil. Add the beans and cook for 5 minutes. Drain the beans and rinse them with cold water.
2. Heat the butter and oil in a frying pan over medium heat. When the butter melts, add the almonds and turn the heat to low. Sauté the almonds until they are lightly browned.
3. Add the beans to the frying pan. Sauté for 5 minutes until the beans are tender. Add salt and pepper to taste.

TOOLS & EQUIPMENT

knife
cutting board
saucepan
strainer
measuring spoons
frying pan
measuring cups
spatula

TRY THIS

You can use a 16-ounce (454-g) package of frozen green beans instead of fresh green beans. Then in step 1, cook the beans for 3 minutes instead of 5 minutes.

GRILLED CORN WITH BUTTER

makes 8 servings

INGREDIENTS

8 ears fresh corn, husks and strings removed

vegetable oil

FOR CHILI LIME BUTTER

½ cup unsalted butter, at room temperature

2 tablespoons fresh lime juice

1 tablespoon chili powder

1 teaspoon ground cumin

1 teaspoon pepper

FOR LEMON HERB BUTTER

½ cup unsalted butter, at room temperature

2 tablespoons fresh lemon juice

1 teaspoon dried basil

1 teaspoon dried oregano

1 teaspoon garlic salt

CHILI LIME BUTTER

LEMON HERB BUTTER

1. Choose a flavored butter recipe to make. Put the butter ingredients in a small bowl. Beat with a fork until well blended.
2. Spread half the flavored butter on the ears of corn. Set the other half aside until serving time.
3. Have an adult helper preheat the grill to medium heat. Lightly grease the grate with oil.
4. Place the buttered corn on the grill and cook for 6 to 8 minutes. Turn the corn often so it cooks evenly and does not burn.
5. Serve hot with the remaining flavored butter.

TOOLS & EQUIPMENT

juicer
measuring spoons
small bowl
fork
grill tongs

TRY THIS

Pick the tastiest type of corn! Look for bright green corn husks. Peel back the husk. Check the kernels. They should be plump and see-through.

SOUPS & STEWS

Fill up your family and friends! Homemade soups and stews are easy and delicious. You can serve them up hot or cold. Soup and stew is great for dinner, lunch, or even breakfast!

Terrific Tortilla Soup

Hearty Heartland Stew

Crowd-Pleasin' Chili

Gulf Coast Gumbo

Three Sisters Soup

Creamy Clam Chowder

CREAMY CLAM CHOWDER

makes 4 servings

INGREDIENTS

- 2 slices bacon, diced
- 1½ cups chopped onion
- 1 teaspoon salt
- ½ teaspoon dried thyme
- 1 garlic clove, minced
- 1½ cups clam juice
- 5 cups peeled and diced potatoes
- 2 tablespoons flour
- 2 10-ounce (283-g) cans chopped clams, with liquid
- 3 cups half-and-half

1. Put the bacon in a frying pan. Cook on medium heat.
2. Flip the bacon with a fork or tongs after 2 minutes. Cook until the bacon is crispy, about 5 minutes.
3. Remove the pan from the heat. Set the bacon on paper towels to drain.
4. Put the bacon, onion, salt, thyme, and garlic in the saucepan. Cook for 4 minutes, stirring constantly.
5. Add the clam juice and potatoes. Cover and cook for 20 minutes.
6. Add the flour, clams, and half-and-half. Bring to a boil. Stir constantly.
7. Cook about 5 more minutes or until thick. Ladle into bowls for you and your friends!

TOOLS & EQUIPMENT

knife
cutting board
peeler
frying pan
fork or tongs
paper towels
measuring cups
measuring spoons
saucepan with lid
mixing spoon
ladle
serving bowls

THREE SISTERS SOUP

makes 6 servings

INGREDIENTS

1 tablespoon olive oil
1 cup diced onion
1 teaspoon garlic salt
2 cups drained canned corn
2 cups green beans
2 cups peeled and cubed yellow squash
1½ cups peeled and cubed potatoes
1 cup of red pepper, diced
5 cups water
1½ tablespoons chicken bouillon granules
2 tablespoons butter, cubed
2 tablespoons flour
½ teaspoon pepper
½ teaspoon cinnamon

1. Heat the oil, onion, and garlic salt in a frying pan on medium heat. Stir and cook for 5 minutes. Remove the pan from heat and set it aside.
2. Put the corn, beans, squash, potatoes, red pepper, and water in a large saucepan. Stir in the bouillon granules.
3. Heat the vegetable mixture in the saucepan on high until it boils. Cook 10 minutes or until the vegetables are soft. Stir constantly.
4. Mix the flour and butter together in a small bowl. Add it to the saucepan. Stir.
5. Turn the heat to medium. Add the onion mixture. Cook 5 minutes, until the soup thickens. Add the pepper and cinnamon.
6. Ladle into bowls for a true feast!

TOOLS & EQUIPMENT

knife
cutting board
peeler
measuring cups
measuring spoons
frying pan
mixing spoons
saucepan
mixing bowl
ladle
serving bowls

FUN FRENCH ONION SOUP

makes 4 servings

INGREDIENTS

- 8 slices of French baguette, each ¼ inch (1.9 cm) thick
- 2 tablespoons olive oil
- 4 large onions, sliced into thin rings
- 4 cups beef broth
- 1 cup grated Swiss cheese
- salt and pepper

1. Preheat the oven to 350 degrees.
2. Put the slices of baguette on a baking sheet. Bake for 5 minutes. Flip the slices over with tongs and bake for 5 more minutes. Remove the slices from the oven and let them cool.
3. Heat the oil in a soup pot. Add the onions and cook over low heat for at least 30 minutes. Use a mixing spoon to mix the onions every few minutes. The onions are ready when they are deep golden brown.
4. Add the broth to the pot. Bring to a boil over high heat. Cover the pot and turn the heat low. Simmer for 20 minutes.
5. Ladle the soup into bowls. Put two slices of baked baguette in each bowl.
6. Sprinkle ¼ cup cheese over each bowl of soup. Serve with salt and pepper.

TOOLS & EQUIPMENT

knife
cutting board
grater
baking sheet
tongs
measuring spoons
soup pot with lid
mixing spoon
measuring cups
ladle
serving bowls

TERRIFIC TORTILLA SOUP

makes 6 to 8 servings

INGREDIENTS

- 2 limes, cut into wedges
- 1 cup sour cream
- ½ cup cilantro leaves
- 1 cup grated Monterey Jack cheese
- 1 avocado, chopped
- 1 tablespoon olive oil
- 1 small white onion, chopped
- 3 cloves garlic, finely chopped
- 1 small can diced green chiles
- 4 cups chicken broth
- 28-ounce (794-g) can diced tomatoes
- ½ teaspoon salt
- ½ teaspoon dried thyme
- 1 teaspoon dried oregano
- 1 teaspoon ground cumin
- 1 tablespoon chili powder
- 2 cups cooked shredded chicken
- 1½ cups tortilla chips, broken into smaller pieces

1. Put the limes, sour cream, cilantro, cheese, and avocado in small bowls. These are the toppings. Set them aside.
2. Heat the oil in a soup pot over medium-high heat. Add the onions and cook for 5 minutes, stirring occasionally.
3. Add the garlic and chiles and cook for 2 minutes.
4. Add the broth, tomatoes, salt, thyme, oregano, cumin, and chili powder. Bring to a boil. Then reduce the heat to low and simmer for 15 minutes.
5. Add the chicken and simmer for 5 minutes.
6. To serve, put some broken tortilla chips in each bowl. Fill the bowls with soup.
7. Put the prepared ingredients from step 1 on the table. Let everyone garnish their own soup with the toppings they like best.

TOOLS & EQUIPMENT

knife	**measuring cups**	**measuring spoons**
cutting board	**small bowls**	**mixing spoon**
grater	**soup pot**	**serving bowls**

CROWD-PLEASIN' CHILI

makes 8 servings

INGREDIENTS

1 pound (0.45 kg) ground beef or ground turkey
1 cup chopped onion
2 cloves garlic, chopped
2 stalks celery, sliced
28-ounce (794-g) can chunky tomato sauce
½ cup water
2 tablespoons chili powder
1 teaspoon salt
½ teaspoon pepper
1 teaspoon sugar
1 teaspoon Worcestershire sauce
15-ounce (425-g) can kidney beans
sour cream
grated cheddar cheese
chopped scallions

1. Cook the meat, onion, and garlic in a 4-quart pot over medium-high heat. Break up the meat with a mixing spoon so it cooks evenly. When all traces of pink are gone from the meat, have an adult helper drain the grease from the pan.
2. Add the celery, tomato sauce, water, chili powder, salt, pepper, sugar, and Worcestershire sauce. Stir to blend. Heat the mixture to boiling, then reduce the heat to low.
3. Cook for about 20 minutes, stirring occasionally.
4. Use a strainer to drain the kidney beans. Rinse the beans well under running water.
5. Add the beans to the pot and increase the heat to medium high. Heat until the mixture boils, then reduce the heat to low.
6. Cook for an additional 20 to 30 minutes, or until the celery is tender.
7. Use a ladle to put chili in bowls. Serve the sour cream, cheese, and scallions on the side, and let your guests add their own garnishes to the chili.

TOOLS & EQUIPMENT

knife
cutting board
grater
measuring cups
4-quart pot
mixing spoon
measuring spoons
strainer
ladle
serving bowls

GULF COAST GUMBO

makes 5 servings

INGREDIENTS

2 tablespoons butter
¼ cup flour
1 green pepper, chopped
1 onion, chopped
3 stalks celery, chopped
2 cups chicken broth
6 tomatoes, diced
2 teaspoons Worcestershire sauce
½ teaspoon thyme
3 garlic cloves, minced
½ cup parsley
½ teaspoon salt
½ teaspoon black pepper
½ cayenne pepper
1 pound (0.45 kg) shrimp, peeled

1. Melt the butter in a large saucepan over medium heat. Stir in the flour. The flour will turn brown and become thicker. Cook for 10 minutes. Turn the heat to low.
2. Add the green pepper, onion, and celery. Stir and cook 15 minutes.
3. Add the chicken broth. Turn the heat to medium.
4. Cook until the broth begins to boil. Stir in the tomatoes, Worcestershire sauce, thyme, garlic, parsley, salt, black pepper, and cayenne pepper.
5. Turn the heat down to low. Cover the pan. Cook 20 minutes.
6. Add the shrimp and stir. Cook 10 minutes. Serve warm.

TOOLS & EQUIPMENT

knife
cutting board
saucepan with lid
measuring cups
mixing spoon
measuring spoons

HEARTY HEARTLAND STEW

makes 8 servings

INGREDIENTS

- ½ cup plus 2 tablespoons butter
- ½ cup flour
- 4 cups water
- ½ cup diced carrots
- 1 cup chopped onion
- ½ cup diced celery
- 1 potato, chopped
- ½ cup peas
- ½ cup corn
- 8-ounce (227-g) can stewed tomatoes
- 6 beef bouillon cubes
- ¼ pound (0.11 kg) round steak, chopped
- ¼ teaspoon pepper
- 2 tablespoons steak sauce

1. Put ½ cup butter in a large saucepan. Heat over medium-high heat. Once the butter is melted, add the flour. Stir constantly until the mixture turns brown. It takes about 5 minutes.
2. Slowly add 2 cups water. Stir until the mixture is smooth.
3. Add the carrots, onion, celery, potato, peas, corn, tomatoes, bouillon, and 2 cups water.
4. Heat until the mixture boils. Then turn the heat to low.
5. Put 2 tablespoons butter in a frying pan. Heat over high heat until it is melted. Add the steak. Cook until the steak pieces are completely brown.
6. Put the cooked steak in the saucepan. Cover and cook over low heat for 90 minutes. Add the pepper and steak sauce.

TOOLS & EQUIPMENT

knife
cutting board
saucepan with lid
measuring cups
mixing spoon
frying pan
measuring spoons

DIPS & DRINKS

Want to make tasty refreshments for friends and family? Whipping up dips and drinks is a great way to start! They are quick and easy. You can serve them up hot or cold.

Dilly & Chilly Dips for Veggies

Seven Layer Dip

Scrumptious Sweet Tea
Watermelon Agua Fresca
¡Olé! Guacamole

¡OLÉ! GUACAMOLE

makes 2 cups

INGREDIENTS

2 very ripe medium avocados
1 small tomato, chopped
½ cup minced white onion
1 tablespoon fresh lime juice
¼ teaspoon salt

1. Cut the avocados in half and remove the pits. Scoop the avocado fruit from the skin and put it in a bowl.
2. Mash the avocado with a fork until it is mostly smooth.
3. Add the other ingredients and stir with the fork until blended. Serve fresh!

TOOLS & EQUIPMENT

knife
cutting board
juicer
spoon
mixing bowl
fork
measuring cup
measuring spoons

SEVEN LAYER DIP

makes 5 servings

INGREDIENTS

- 1-ounce (28-g) package taco seasoning
- 16-ounce (454-g) can refried beans
- ½ cup grated pepper jack cheese
- ½ cup grated cheddar cheese
- 8 ounces (227 g) sour cream
- 1 cup guacamole
- 2 tomatoes, diced
- 1 cup chunky salsa
- 1 cup diced green onions
- tortilla chips

1. Mix the taco seasoning and beans together in a small bowl.
2. Mix the cheeses in a separate small bowl.
3. Put about 2 tablespoons of the bean mixture in each glass. Put 2 tablespoons of sour cream on top of the beans. Put 2 tablespoons of guacamole on top of the sour cream.
4. Put 2 tablespoons of chopped tomatoes on top of the guacamole in each glass. Drain the extra liquid out of the salsa. Put 2 tablespoons of salsa on top of the tomatoes. Put 2 tablespoons of the cheese mixture on top of the salsa.
5. Sprinkle green onions on top of the cheese.
6. Serve with tortilla chips for dipping.

TOOLS & EQUIPMENT

knife
cutting board
grater
mixing bowls
mixing spoon
measuring cups
measuring spoons
5 clear serving glasses

DILLY & CHILLY DIPS FOR VEGGIES

makes 2 cups

INGREDIENTS

FOR DILLY DIP

1 cup sour cream
1 cup plain yogurt
¼ cup minced white onion
2 teaspoons dried dill weed
½ teaspoon salt

FOR CHILLY DIP

1 cup sour cream
1 cup plain yogurt
4 scallions, chopped
1½ teaspoons chili powder
½ teaspoon garlic powder
½ teaspoon salt

OPTIONAL SIDES

baby carrots
celery
green pepper
broccoli
cauliflower
cucumber
jicama

TOOLS & EQUIPMENT

knife
cutting board
measuring cups
measuring spoons
small mixing bowls
mixing spoons
serving platter

1. To make either dip, mix all the ingredients together until they are well blended.
2. Put the dip in a bowl and place it on a serving platter. Surround the bowl of dip with vegetables such as baby carrots, celery, green pepper, broccoli, cauliflower, cucumber, and jicama.

TRY THIS

If you like your dip more dilly, add another teaspoon of dill weed. For extra chilly dip, add another teaspoon of chili powder. For a thicker dip, use only sour cream instead of a yogurt and sour cream mixture.

CARAMELIZED ONION DIP

makes 2½ cups

INGREDIENTS

- 2 tablespoons olive oil
- 2 large onions, cut in half top to bottom and thinly sliced
- 1 teaspoon sugar
- 1 tablespoon balsamic vinegar
- 1 cup sour cream
- ½ cup mayonnaise
- ½ teaspoon Worcestershire sauce
- salt and pepper

1. Heat the oil in a large saucepan over medium-high heat. Add the onions. Turn the heat to low. Cook until the onions turn light brown, stirring occasionally. This can take 30 minutes or more.
2. Add the sugar and balsamic vinegar. Continue cooking over low heat until the onions are a deep caramel color. Let the onions cool.
3. Stir the onion mixture, sour cream, and mayonnaise together in a medium mixing bowl.
4. Stir in the Worcestershire sauce and salt and pepper to taste.

TOOLS & EQUIPMENT

knife
cutting board
measuring cups
saucepan
mixing spoon
mixing bowl
measuring cups
silicone spatula

SCRUMPTIOUS SWEET TEA

makes 8 servings

INGREDIENTS

8 cups water
6 tea bags
⅛ teaspoon baking soda
1 cup sugar
ice
1 orange, sliced
mint leaves

1. Put 2 cups of water in a saucepan. Heat the water on high.
2. When the water boils, turn off the stove. Put the tea bags and baking soda in the saucepan. Cover the pan. Let it sit for 15 minutes.
3. Take out the tea bags with a spoon. Pour the tea into a large pitcher. Stir in the sugar slowly until it dissolves.
4. Add 6 cups of cold water. Stir.
5. Pour the tea in glasses over ice. Add an orange slice and a few mint leaves to each glass.

TOOLS & EQUIPMENT

knife
cutting board
measuring cups
saucepan with lid
measuring spoon
mixing spoon
large pitcher
drinking glasses

WATERMELON AGUA FRESCA

makes 8 servings

INGREDIENTS

1 cup sugar
1 cup water
6 cups cubed seedless watermelon
ice
1 lime, cut into wedges

1. Combine the sugar and water in a small saucepan. Bring to a boil and stir until the sugar dissolves. Remove from heat and cool for 30 minutes.
2. Put half the watermelon and half the sugar mixture in a blender. Blend until smooth. Pour it into the pitcher. Repeat with the remaining watermelon and sugar mixture.
3. Stir well. Pour the drink into glasses filled with ice. Garnish with wedges of lime.

TOOLS & EQUIPMENT

knife
cutting board
measuring cup
saucepan
mixing spoon
blender
2-quart pitcher
drinking glasses

FRESH-SQUEEZED LEMONADE

makes 2 quarts

INGREDIENTS

1 cup sugar
6 to 8 lemons
water
ice

1. Make a simple syrup. Put the sugar and 1 cup of water in a small saucepan. Bring it to a boil and stir until the sugar dissolves.
2. Remove the pan from the heat. Let the syrup cool for 30 minutes. Add zest from 4 lemons. Refrigerate overnight.
3. Strain the syrup into a pitcher.
4. Juice the lemons until you have 1 cup of fresh lemon juice. Put the lemon juice in the pitcher. Add water to fill the pitcher. Stir. If the lemonade is too sour, add more sugar and stir until the sugar dissolves.
5. Serve in glasses with ice and lemon slices.

TOOLS & EQUIPMENT

measuring cups
saucepan
mixing spoon
zester or grater
strainer
2-quart pitcher
knife
cutting board
juicer
drinking glasses

DESSERTS

Surprise your friends and family by making homemade desserts! Homemade desserts are special treats. They taste and smell great. Try making cake, pie, cookies, and more!

Classy Molasses Cookies

Moist & Delicious Butter Cake

Berry Frozen Fruit Pops

Nummy Nut Wedges

Blueberry Crumb Cake

Kickin' Chili Brownies

DESSERTS

ICE CREAM & COOKIES PIE

makes 10 servings

INGREDIENTS

- 3 tablespoons butter
- 22 cream-filled chocolate cookies
- ⅛ teaspoon salt
- ¼ teaspoon peppermint extract
- 1 quart mint chocolate ice cream
- 1 cup hot fudge

TOOLS & EQUIPMENT

- glass measuring cup
- food processor
- measuring spoons
- mixing bowl
- fork
- 9-inch pie dish
- plastic wrap
- ice cream scoop
- silicone spatula
- plates

1. Preheat the oven to 350 degrees.
2. Put the butter in the glass measuring cup. Microwave it on high for 30 seconds. If it is not completely melted, heat it for an additional 15 seconds. Set it aside to cool.
3. Put the cookies and the salt in a food processor. Use the pulse button or quickly turn the machine on and off until the cookies are finely ground.

4. Put the ground cookies in a mixing bowl and add the slightly cooled butter and peppermint extract. Mix and mash with a fork until everything is well blended.
5. Press the mixture into a pie dish, making an even layer that covers the bottom and sides of the pie dish.
6. Bake the crust for 6 to 8 minutes. Remove it from the oven and let it cool completely.
7. Cover the crust with plastic wrap and freeze it until you are ready to fill it.
8. When you are ready to fill the crust, remove the ice cream from the freezer and let it soften slightly. To soften ice cream in a microwave, use high power for about 10 seconds.
9. Scoop the ice cream into the crust and spread it evenly with a silicone spatula. Return the pie to the freezer for 2 to 3 hours, or until the ice cream is firm.
10. To serve the pie, remove it from the freezer and let it sit for about 10 minutes. Drizzle hot fudge over the top. Slice the pie into wedges and put them on plates.

BERRY FROZEN FRUIT POPS

makes 4 fruit pops

INGREDIENTS

- 1½ cups raspberry yogurt
- 2 tablespoons raspberry syrup
- 1 cup fresh raspberries

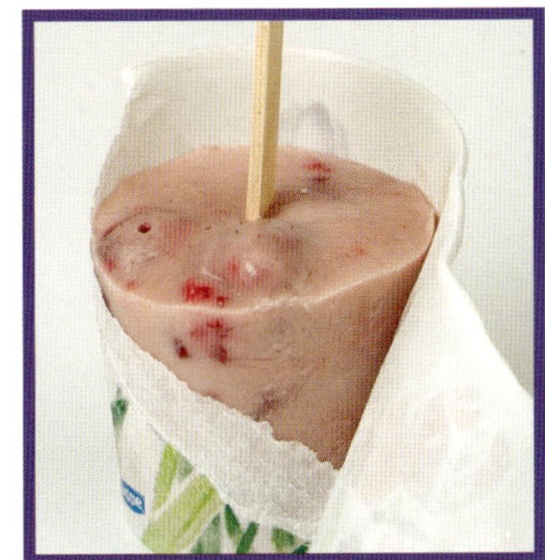

1. Mix the yogurt and syrup together until they are blended. Gently fold in the raspberries.
2. Distribute the mixture evenly into the paper cups. Put a wooden craft stick in the middle of each cup.
3. Place the cups in the freezer for 6 to 8 hours. If you make these in the evening, they will be ready for after-school snacking the next day.
4. Tear the paper cup away from the frozen pop and enjoy!

TOOLS & EQUIPMENT

measuring cups
measuring spoons
small mixing bowl
silicone spatula
4 5-ounce (142-g) waxed paper cups
4 wooden craft sticks

TRY THIS

Make two-tone berry pops. Make a raspberry yogurt mixture and a blueberry yogurt mixture. Distribute either mixture evenly among 8 waxed paper cups, filling each cup about halfway. Then finish filling the cups with the other mixture. Put in the sticks and freeze as in step 3 above. This cool alternative makes 8 pops.

OVER-THE-TOP APPLE CRISP

makes 6 servings

INGREDIENTS

2 pounds (0.9 kg) Granny Smith apples (about 4 or 5), peeled, cored, and thinly sliced

juice of ½ lemon

¼ cup water

½ cup sugar

½ cup brown sugar

1 teaspoon cinnamon

¼ teaspoon salt

¾ cup flour

1 stick butter, cut into 8 pieces

1. Preheat the oven to 350 degrees.
2. Put the apples in the baking pan. They might be higher than the top of the pan. Don't worry, they will shrink as they bake.
3. Strain the lemon juice and mix it with the water. Pour the mixture evenly over the apples.
4. Put the rest of the ingredients in a large mixing bowl. Use your clean hands to rub the butter into the dry ingredients.
5. Sprinkle the mixture evenly over the apples but don't mix the two together.
6. Cover the pan loosely with aluminum foil and put it in the oven. Bake for 25 minutes and then remove the foil. Bake for another 35 minutes, or until the topping is golden brown.

TOOLS & EQUIPMENT

peeler
corer
knife
cutting board
juicer
8 × 8-inch baking pan
strainer
measuring cups
mixing bowls
mixing spoon
measuring spoons
aluminum foil

CLASSY MOLASSES COOKIES

makes 36 cookies

INGREDIENTS

- ¾ cup butter
- 1 egg
- 1½ cups sugar
- ¾ cup dark molasses
- 2 cups flour
- 1 teaspoon salt
- 1 teaspoon baking soda
- 1½ teaspoons ground ginger
- ½ teaspoon ground cloves
- ½ teaspoon nutmeg
- ¼ teaspoon allspice
- non-stick cooking spray

1. Put the butter, egg, and 1 cup of sugar in a large mixing bowl. Beat with the electric mixer. Add the molasses. Beat until smooth.
2. Put the flour, salt, baking soda, ginger, cloves, nutmeg, and allspice in a medium mixing bowl. Whisk them together. Pour the flour mixture into the molasses mixture. Stir well. Put the dough in the refrigerator for 1 hour.
3. Preheat the oven to 375 degrees. Grease the baking sheet with non-stick cooking spray.
4. Remove the dough from the refrigerator. Sprinkle flour on your hands. Roll the dough into small balls. Roll each ball in sugar.
5. Place the balls of dough on the baking sheet. Flatten them with a fork. Bake for 12 minutes. Let the cookies cool.

TOOLS & EQUIPMENT

measuring cups
mixing bowls
electric mixer
measuring spoons
whisk
baking sheet
fork

NEW ORLEANS BEIGNETS

makes 25 beignets

INGREDIENTS

- 2¾ cups flour
- ½ cup sugar
- 2 teaspoons baking powder
- ½ teaspoon baking soda
- ½ teaspoon salt
- 1 cup buttermilk
- 1 egg
- 1 teaspoon vanilla extract
- ⅓ cup water
- 3 cups vegetable oil
- ¼ cup powdered sugar

1. Put the flour, sugar, baking powder, baking soda, and salt in a medium mixing bowl. Stir and set the bowl aside.
2. Put the buttermilk, egg, vanilla extract, and water in a large mixing bowl. Whisk well. Add the flour mixture to the buttermilk mixture. Stir until doughy.
3. Sprinkle flour on a clean work surface. Place the dough on the flour. Sprinkle flour on your hands. Lightly knead the dough. Flatten the dough into a square with your hands. Cover a knife with flour. Cut the dough into 2-inch (5-cm) squares.
4. Put the oil in a large frying pan. Heat the oil to 325 degrees. Use a slotted spoon to lower the dough squares into the oil.
5. Cook one side for 3 minutes. Use the slotted spoon to flip them over. Cook for another 3 minutes.
6. Use the slotted spoon to remove the beignets. Put them on paper towels. Sprinkle powdered sugar on top.

TOOLS & EQUIPMENT

measuring cups
measuring spoons
mixing bowls
mixing spoon
whisk
knife
frying pan
fryer thermometer
slotted spoon
paper towels

MOIST & DELICIOUS BUTTER CAKE

makes 24 servings

INGREDIENTS

- non-stick cooking spray
- 1 cup butter
- ¼ cup milk
- 4 eggs
- 18.25-ounce (517-g) package yellow cake mix
- 8 ounces (227 g) cream cheese
- 2 cups powdered sugar
- ½ cup blueberries

1. Preheat the oven to 350 degrees. Grease the baking dish with non-stick cooking spray.
2. Put the butter, milk, and 2 eggs in a large mixing bowl. Beat together with the electric mixer. Stir in the cake mix. Pour the batter evenly into the baking dish.
3. Put the cream cheese and 2 eggs in a medium mixing bowl. Beat together with the electric mixer. Slowly add the powdered sugar. Mix well.
4. Pour the cream cheese mixture evenly over the cake batter. Bake for 35 minutes, or until the top starts to brown. Stick a toothpick in the cake. When it comes out clean, the cake is done. Take the cake out and let it cool. Serve it with powdered sugar and blueberries.

TOOLS & EQUIPMENT

- 9 × 13-inch baking dish
- measuring cups
- mixing bowls
- electric mixer
- mixing spoon
- toothpick

NUMMY NUT WEDGES

makes 8 to 10 servings

INGREDIENTS

- 1 package pie crust mix (for 2 crusts)
- ½ cup sugar
- 3 to 4 tablespoons water
- flour
- 1 cup walnuts, finely chopped
- 2 tablespoons honey
- 1 teaspoon cinnamon
- 1 teaspoon lemon juice
- milk
- ½ cup semisweet chocolate pieces
- 1 teaspoon butter

TOOLS & EQUIPMENT

- knife
- cutting board
- juicer
- measuring cups
- mixing bowls
- measuring spoons
- mixing spoon
- rolling pin
- 9-inch round pie dish
- fork
- pastry brush
- wire rack
- saucepan

1. Preheat the oven to 375 degrees.
2. In a medium bowl, stir together pie crust mix and ¼ cup sugar. Add enough water to form a ball of dough. Divide the dough in half.
3. Sprinkle a little flour onto the counter. Roll each half of the dough into a 9-inch (23-cm) circle. Put one of the circles on an ungreased round pie dish.
4. Combine the walnuts, ¼ cup of sugar, honey, cinnamon, and lemon juice in a bowl.
5. Spread the nut mixture over the dough in the round pie dish. Put the other dough circle on top.
6. Use the tines of a fork to press around the edges of the dough. Prick the top of the dough with a fork. Brush it with milk.
7. Bake for 15 to 20 minutes or until pastry starts to brown. Put the pie on a wire rack.
8. Combine the chocolate pieces and butter in a small saucepan. Cook and stir over low heat just until melted.
9. Drizzle the chocolate over the warm pie. Cut the pie into 8 to 10 wedges. Let them cool completely before serving.

BLUEBERRY CRUMB CAKE

makes 9 servings

INGREDIENTS

- 10 tablespoons butter, plus extra
- 2 cups all-purpose flour, plus extra
- 1 cup sugar
- ½ cup brown sugar
- 1 teaspoon salt
- 1 teaspoon cinnamon
- 2 beaten eggs
- ⅔ cup milk
- 1 cup fresh or frozen blueberries

1. Preheat the oven to 350 degrees. Grease the baking dish with butter. Sprinkle flour over the inside of the dish. Turn the dish upside down to remove any extra flour.
2. Combine the flour, sugars, salt, and cinnamon in a large mixing bowl. Using the pastry blender, cut in butter until the mixture looks like big crumbs. Set aside ¾ cup of the mixture in a small mixing bowl. This will be used for the topping.
3. Whisk the eggs and milk together in a small mixing bowl. Stir it into the crumb mixture in the large mixing bowl.
4. Spread the batter in the baking dish. Arrange the blueberries evenly over the batter. Sprinkle the crumb mixture from the small bowl over the top.
5. Bake for 30 minutes. Stick a toothpick into the center of the cake. If it comes out clean, the cake is done. If not, bake for a few more minutes and test again.

TOOLS & EQUIPMENT

9 × 9-inch baking dish
measuring cups
measuring spoons
mixing bowls
mixing spoon
pastry blender
whisk
toothpick

KICKIN' CHILI BROWNIES

makes 32 brownies

INGREDIENTS

- 1 cup butter, plus extra
- 4 ounces (113 g) unsweetened baking chocolate
- 2 cups sugar
- ½ teaspoon salt
- ½ teaspoon baking powder
- 1 cup flour, plus extra
- 2 tablespoons chili powder
- 2 tablespoons cinnamon
- 1 teaspoon vanilla extract
- 4 eggs, lightly beaten with a fork

1. Preheat the oven to 350 degrees. Grease the baking dish with butter. Sprinkle flour over the inside of the dish. Turn the dish upside down to remove any extra flour.
2. Put the chocolate and butter in a microwave-safe bowl. Cook for 1 minute on high. Take it out and stir it. If the chocolate isn't melted, cook for 30 seconds more. Stir again until the chocolate is completely melted.
3. Mix the sugar, salt, baking powder, flour, chili powder, and cinnamon in a large bowl.
4. Add the chocolate mixture, vanilla extract, and eggs. Mix well.
5. Spread the batter evenly in the baking dish.
6. Bake for 30 to 35 minutes. Insert a toothpick into the brownies. If it comes out clean, the brownies are done.

TOOLS & EQUIPMENT

fork
9 × 13-inch baking dish
measuring cups
microwave-safe bowl
mixing spoon
measuring spoons
mixing bowl
silicone spatula
toothpick

CHOCOLATE HOT LAVA CAKES

makes 4 servings

INGREDIENTS

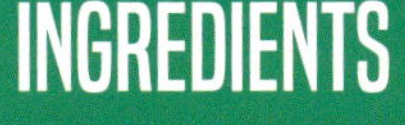

- ½ cup butter, plus extra
- 4 ounces (113 g) semisweet chocolate
- 1 tablespoon milk
- 1 teaspoon vanilla extract
- 1 cup powdered sugar
- 2 eggs plus 1 egg yolk
- 6 tablespoons flour
- 1 teaspoon cinnamon

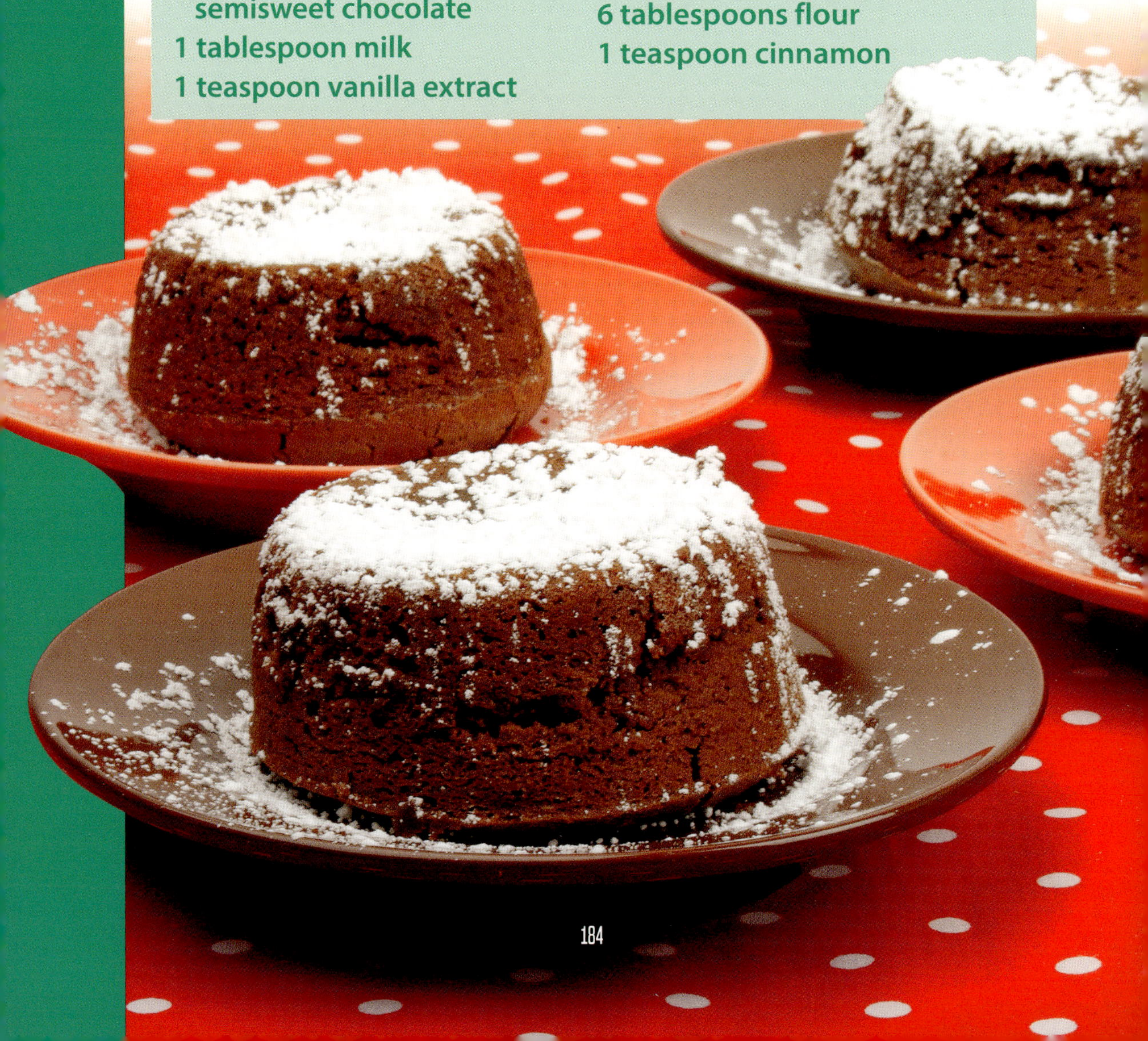

1. Preheat the oven to 425 degrees. Grease each custard cup with butter. Place them on the baking sheet.
2. Put the chocolate and ½ cup butter in a microwave-safe bowl. Microwave on high for 1 minute, or until butter is melted. Stir with a whisk until well blended.
3. Add the milk, vanilla extract, and 1 cup of powdered sugar. Whisk together.
4. Add the eggs and yolk. Whisk until well blended. Add the flour and cinnamon. Whisk until the mixture is completely blended and smooth. Pour into the custard cups.
5. Bake 13 to 15 minutes or until the sides and center are firm. Let them cool for 1 minute. Run a table knife around the edges of the cakes. Put a small plate upside down over a cake. Turn the cake and plate over together. Shake gently so the cake falls onto the plate. Repeat with the other cakes. Sprinkle the cakes with powdered sugar.

TRY THIS

For spiced lava cakes, replace the cinnamon with ½ teaspoon ground ginger and a pinch of ground cloves or allspice.

TOOLS & EQUIPMENT

4 6-ounce (170-g) custard cups or mini soufflé dishes
baking sheet
measuring cups
microwave-safe bowl
whisk
measuring spoons
table knife
small plates

NUTTY GOODNESS PECAN PIE

makes 8 servings

INGREDIENTS

- 9-inch (23-cm) uncooked pie crust
- ½ cup butter
- 2 eggs, at room temperature
- 1 cup brown sugar
- ¼ cup sugar
- 1 tablespoon flour
- 1 tablespoon milk
- 1 teaspoon vanilla extract
- 1½ cups chopped pecans

1. Preheat the oven to 400 degrees.
2. Place the pie crust in the pie plate. Press lightly to fit it into the bottom of the plate. Trim the edge evenly around the pie plate. Pinch the edge to form a rim around the pie.
3. Use a fork to poke some holes in the bottom of the pie crust.
4. Melt the butter in a microwave-safe bowl.
5. Crack the eggs into a large mixing bowl. Beat them with an electric mixer. When the eggs are foamy, mix in the butter. Add the sugars, flour, milk, and vanilla extract. Mix well.
6. Add the pecans. Gently stir them into the mixture.
7. Pour the mixture into the pie crust. Bake for 10 minutes. Turn the oven temperature down to 300 degrees. Bake for 45 to 55 minutes until firm.

TRY THIS

Put a baking sheet on the bottom rack of the oven. It will catch any drips from the pie as it bakes.

TOOLS & EQUIPMENT

knife
cutting board
pie plate
fork
measuring cups
microwave-safe bowl
mixing bowl
electric mixer
measuring spoons
mixing spoon

GLOSSARY

bacteria
tiny, one-celled organisms that can only be seen through a microscope.

dissolve
to become part of a liquid.

dressing
a sauce that is used in salads.

extract
a product made by concentrating the juices taken from something such as a plant.

garnish
something used to decorate food or drink.

insert
to put something into something else.

kernel
a grain or seed of a plant such as corn, wheat, or oats.

pastry
a sweet, baked food.

patty
a round, flat cake made with chopped food.

puree
food that is finely ground to make a paste or a thick liquid.

serrated
having a jagged edge.

skewer
a long, thin piece of wood or metal used to pierce and hold food.

thaw
to melt or unfreeze.

yolk
the yellow inner portion of a bird or reptile egg.

TO LEARN MORE

FURTHER READINGS

The Complete Cookbook for Teen Chefs. America's Test Kitchen, 2022.

Dahle, Tiffany. *The Totally Awesome Ultimate Kids' Cookbook: Simple Recipes & Fun Skills to Cook Fabulous Meals for Your Family*. Page Street Publishing, 2023.

Lake, Theia. *Creating in the Kitchen*. PowerKids, 2024.

ONLINE RESOURCES

To learn more about cooking, please visit **abdobooklinks.com** or scan this QR code. These links are routinely monitored and updated to provide the most current information available.

INDEX

PHOTO CREDITS

Cover Photographs: Mighty Media, Inc.

Interior Photographs: Charles B. Ming Onn/Shutterstock Images, p. 99 (bottom); chrisbrignell/Shutterstock Images, p. 14 (bottom); fredredhat/Shutterstock Images, p. 16 (top); Ivaschenko Roman/Shutterstock Images, p. 145 (bottom); Maks Narodenko/Shutterstock Images, p. 162; Mighty Media Inc., pp. 1, 2, 3, 4, 5, 6, 7, 8, 11, 12 (top, bottom), 13, 14 (top, second from top, second from bottom), 15, 16 (second from top, second from bottom, bottom), 17, 18, 19 (second from top, middle, bottom, second from bottom), 20, 21, 22, 23, 24, 25, 26, 27, 28-29, 30, 31, 32-33, 34, 35, 36, 37, 38, 39, 40, 41, 42, 43, 44-45, 46-47, 48, 49, 50, 51, 52, 53, 54, 55, 56, 57, 58, 59, 61, 62, 63, 64-65, 66, 67, 68, 69 (top), 70, 71 (top), 72, 73 (top), 74, 75, 76, 77, 78, 79, 80, 81, 83, 84, 85, 86, 87 (right), 88, 89, 90, 91, 92, 93, 94, 95, 96-97, 98, 99 (top), 100, 101, 102, 103, 104, 105, 106, 107, 108, 109, 110, 111, 112, 113 (top), 114, 115 (top, bottom right), 116, 117, 118, 119, 120, 121, 122, 123, 124, 125, 126, 127, 128, 129, 130, 131, 132, 133, 134, 135, 136, 137, 138, 139, 140, 141, 142, 143, 144, 145 (top), 146, 147, 148-149, 150-151, 152, 153 (top), 154, 155, 156, 157, 158, 159, 160, 161 (top), 162-163, 164-165, 166, 167, 168, 169, 170, 171,172, 173, 174, 175, 176, 177, 178, 179, 180, 181, 182, 183, 184, 185, 186, 187; pamela_d_mcadams/Adobe Stock, p. 161 (bottom); ravl/Shutterstock Images, p. 115 (bottom left); Shutterstock Images, pp. 9, 12 (middle), 19 (top), 69 (bottom), 71 (bottom), 73 (bottom), 113 (bottom); steamroller_blues/Shutterstock Images, p. 87 (left); V_S/Shutterstock Images, p. 153 (bottom)

Design Elements: Mighty Media, Inc.

ABDOBOOKS.COM
Published by Abdo Reference, a division of ABDO, PO Box 398166, Minneapolis, Minnesota 55439.

Printed in China
052024
092024

Editor: Jessica Rusick
Series Designer: Colleen McLaren
Production Designer: Mighty Media, Inc.

LIBRARY OF CONGRESS CONTROL NUMBER: 2023949529

PUBLISHER'S CATALOGING-IN-PUBLICATION DATA
Names: Schrader, Zoey, author.
Title: The cooking encyclopedia / by Zoey Schrader
Description: Minneapolis, Minnesota : Abdo Reference, 2025 | Series: Makerspace encyclopedias | Includes online resources and index.
Identifiers: ISBN 9781098294373 (lib. bdg.) | ISBN 9798384913641 (ebook)
Subjects: LCSH: Cooking--Juvenile literature. | Cookery--Juvenile literature. | Food preparation--Juvenile literature. | Cuisine--Juvenile literature. | Food--Juvenile literature. | Encyclopedias and dictionaries--Juvenile literature.
Classification: DDC 641.7--dc23